KAZAT AKMATOV

Bishkek, January 2010

MUNABIYA

HERTFORDSHIRE PRESS

Published in United Kindom
Hertforfshire Press © 2013
(Imprint of Silk Road Media)
Suite 125, 43 Bedford Street
Covent Garden, London
WC2 9HA United Kingdom
www.hertfordshirepress.com

Design by Aleksandra Vlasova
Cover Illustration by Varvara Perekrest
Translated from Kyrgyz to Russian by Sabyrbek Kuruchbekov
Translated from Russian to English by Elizabeth Adams
Edited by Laura Hamilton

British Library Catalogue in Publication Data
A catalogue record for this book is available from the British Library
Library of Congress in Publication Data
A catalogue record for this book has been requested

ISBN: 978-0-9574807-5-9

MUNABIYA

KAZAT AKMATOV

Bishkek, January 2010

Contents

Foreword 11
Munabiya 13
Shahidka 51

MUNABIYA

KAZAT AKMATOV

Bishkek, January 2010

Kazat Akmatov was born at the beginning of the World War II, in Bosteri in the Kyrgyz Republic of the Soviet Union. Both his own father and his adoptive father perished and hence, locals named the young orphan Kazat, meaning war or fight. His talent as a narrator emerged early and when he was between ten and twelve, he was punished at school for detaining his classmates with his stories. At fifteen he was commissioned to write a play for his school. The Rich Landowner and the Day Labourers was applauded, although its high standard led parents to suspect that it had been plagiarized from work by Soviet writers on class struggle.

While studying journalism, Akmatov confined his poetry to notebooks, believing that serious subject matter was better presented in prose. Having already worked for the Komsomol (the youth division of the All-Union Communist party) and served as an officer in the Soviet army, he was committed to a career as a writer after finishing University. Instead, he was ordered to join the army by the USSR's Minister of Defense, purportedly to strengthen the ranks. KGB spies had long suspected him of being a nationalist and "immature" communist and the Party organization of the military part of the "Guards" within the Central Asian Military District raised the exclusion of Lieutenant Akmatov from the Communist Party. He was recognized as guilty for asking: "How much time does it take to declassify documents in the Soviet Union, in accordance with the law?"

As a consequence, his first novel Two Strings of Life was not published until 1972. Successful on many levels, it entered the Party's stream of criticism against corrupt officials from the Soviet economic organs. Akmatov was awarded the Nikolai Ostrovsky Prize: the most prestigious accolade for young writers of the USSR. The next stage in Akmatov's oeuvre, characterized by novels Earth Time and Years around the Sun as well as the play, Night of Divorce, proved life-changing. All three works were imbued with the author's compassion for the tragic fate of Kyrgyz people. The media however, submissive to taunts by the Communist Party, printed a series of derogatory articles. Examined by the Central Committee of the Communist Party, Earth Time was declared "anti-Russian" and Years around the Sun,"anti-Soviet". Night of Divorce was pronounced to be "anti-Party", and the Ministry of Culture closed the play and even set alight the props. The author felt attacked from all sides: he was fired from his job in journalism; his books were withdrawn from sale, and the Party ensured that he received none of the high awards and prizes which he had won. No-one would publish Kazat Akmatov.

In retaliation, Akmatov publicly announced his withdrawal from the Communist Party and began to organize the Democratic Movement of Kyrgyzstan. This movement which demanded the separation of Kyrgyzstan from the Soviet Union, the elimination of the Communist Party in Kyrgyzstan and the declaration of independence for Kyrgyzstan, came to fruition in 1991.

After five years in politics as a Member of Parliament, Akmatov returned to writing and much of his work is now published in many languages. His novel Arhat, available in five languages, has won several international prizes and the State Prize of Kyrgyzstan.

Thirteen Steps towards the Fate of Erika Klaus has been well acclaimed. Based on a true incident, it follows the tragic fate of an extraordinary and naïve young Norwegian woman, who arrives in Kyrgyzstan as a Peace Corps volunteer. Set in a remote outpost, where a fascist hide-out has emerged from the ruins of the former Soviet Union, this work explores the daily brutality faced by both Klaus and as significantly, the Kyrgyz people around her .

A writer rather than a politician, Akmatov nevertheless, continues to raise awareness of the oppression of basic human rights throughout Asia and following his description of the brutal regime in Chet, his new novel Shahidka highlights the fate of the Chechen nation and its eternal fight for freedom through a love story between a young Chechen man and a young Russian woman.

Foreword

Our daughter Munabiya was named after the main character of my novel, which was written before she was born. This literary character was loved by readers and our baby, Munashka, was more than worthy to carry her name.

It is said that there are no happy endings, just happy days and happy moments. Happy days filled the eighteen years that we shared with our daughter, illuminating our bond with her and her future.

Oh, dearly loved daughter!
Like a flash of light you disappeared from our home
When you hurriedly left for the next world
Your radiance, the beating of your heart
Fell silent in the life of your family
It can never be the same home without you
Even if it is open wide to fortune
We too will come to the eternal life and to you
Our love will show us the way only to you, to you

Mommy and Daddy

Bishkek – 1987

We can tell ourselves that a lapse in our responsibility and indifference towards those we love is harmless, not worth bothering about, but when life suddenly punishes us, we realize that the punishment was earned. Then, like someone who has been given a wake- up call, you raise your head above the daily grind and realize with belated regret and perhaps a twinge of conscience that you neglected to do your duty. Eyes open, you drop everything and race off to attend to those unavoidable responsibilities that await you.

That was exactly my state of mind as I drove home to my father's house in the village. Worried and distressed, I turned off the radio and rolled up all the windows. My palms grew sweatier against the steering wheel and I experienced an unpleasant sensation of feeling like I had been drenched with dirty water. When anyone descends to that level of gloom, it is difficult to extricate the soul and set it back on a happy course. That was what had happened it me. It was right there, in front of my face, lingering like a speck of dirt in my eye. It was as though I had flagged it up in spite of myself, to sharpen the pain and torture my conscience.

I was already a long way out of the city when I finally grabbed the ill-fated envelope, shoved it into the glove compartment and slammed the door shut. Let it lie there amongst other random stuff. That is where it belongs! I tried to placate myself, as if I were a small child.

There were few cars on the road. I pressed the accelerator lightly and felt my speed pick up. No sooner had I begun to enjoy that simple sensation, than I felt the venomous words of the letter creep back into my mind. When I had read them the first time, my heart was shocked by their absurd unfairness: "It has been two years since your mother died... And you, Januzak's five healthy, grown up sons, have left your father all alone in an empty house. You left a poor, defenseless old man under the heel of that crafty witch Munabiya. The shameless woman has taken everything your mother left behind and dragged it all into her own house. The embers of your hearth, which brimmed over with comfort and happiness when your mother was alive, will be stamped out and shaken into the wind by that damned Munabiya!" The childish script shamed and accused us of inexcusable callousness towards our own father. There was no name or signature of any kind at the end of the letter. Never in my life had I heard words like those contained in that letter and I was appalled. It was repellent to say the least. Only a completely uncivilized person lacking in any sense of fairness could slander and malign us in such a manner.

At first, I had no intention of taking the letter seriously or reproaching myself about anything. My selfish egotism would not allow it. But later, when I had calmly assessed the whole situation, I admitted that it really had been over two years since we buried Mama, and my father had been living all alone in our empty house the whole time. It would not have been so bad if there had been someone with him.

Our father had never so much as ironed a shirt or got dressed by himself. He had worked as a jeweller from an early age and was considered a true master craftsman by everyone in the region. I suppose he used his skillful creations to convey all his thoughts, dreams and moments of joy. The jewellery he made seemed to embody his whole life. Watching him at work, you couldn't help but notice how his eyes flashed and how radiant his face became. He was like a man absorbed by hidden thoughts and secret dreams. For days at a time, we took turns in working the bellows in his workshop, and he spent days at a time in his own world, a world that was closed to us, often without uttering a single word.

Because of this, the people in our aul[1], who only saw Father from the outside, called him Quiet Januzak. They assumed that he took no interest in what went on around him and they barely even mentioned his name when they gathered to make decisions on matters of any importance to the aul.

I found myself thinking what a very strange man he was. He could at least have told us he needed help. My intention was to offload onto my father, part of the guilt I felt for his grim and enforced isolation. After all, why had he never mentioned anything to us? As for me, I was a typical city dweller with a demanding job, who spends so much time dealing with crises at work that there just isn't any time left for family. Nothing but work from morning until night. It's enough to make you forget your father's name, or forget that you even have a father.

The farther I got from the city, the more disorganized my anxious thoughts became. I did my best to plan how I would launch into my excuse and how I would back it up. But the main purpose of my trip was clear; I would have to take my father back to the city with me. Last year my father's relatives had made a sensible suggestion: "Take your father back to the city so he'll be warm and comfortable over the winter. Whilst he's

---

1 Aul : village

15

there, we'll find the right kind of old woman for him and bring them together formally. Then in the spring they can come back to the aul to live." I had seen this as a reasonable piece of advice, but my father wanted to stay at home and there didn't seem to be any suitable candidates, meaning unmarried elderly women, living in the village. I had heard stories of this kind before; someone was always looking for an old woman to take care of yet another old widower but couldn't find the right one. That was when I remembered Munabiya. We never talked to her, even though our houses were on the same street. As far back as I can remember she had always lived alone, in isolation. She had been in conflict with Mama for many years. My deceased mother had hated her more than anyone in the world. We, her beloved children, knew nothing about the reason for her hatred and we made no effort to find out. Ever since we were small we had heard nothing good about Munabiya from our mother.

"That witch hates us. She's destroyed the happiness in our home. I hope she rots, that harpy…" and on and on. Mama never tired of using such words about Munabiya.

I remember something that happened when we were still young. We heard that some women were fighting at a feast. That promised to be interesting, so a gang of us curious boys ran over to watch. When we got there, I saw Mama with her strong hands full of Munabiya's hair, trying to drag the woman by the head. Mama's face burned with fury, as if she were avenging herself on a murderer. Munabiya was younger than Mama and very strong, but she did not fight back. Instead, she tried only to free herself from Mama's grasp. For some reason, most of the onlookers sided with Mama and showed no pity for the defenseless Munabiya. The crowd was drunk and openly enjoying the fight. Whenever someone tried to pull the women apart, people would call out, "Leave them alone. They'll stop when they're tired."

I think my filial pride was hurt. I ran over and shoved Munabiya as she struggled to get away from Mama. People laughed. The crowd was delighted.

"Here comes help from your son!"

"Grab Munabiya by the leg!"

"Rip her skirt off!"

Everyone was voraciously enjoying the sight of me, a naïve little boy egged on by adults, attacking Munabiya after my mother had already humiliated her. Thinking back, I can see that Munabiya was a powerful, good-looking woman, much younger than Mama. If she even noticed the blows from my fists, their impact would have felt as slight as that of a fly. She managed to block my blows with her hands, being careful not to hurt the stupid little creature that was harassing her.

Just when things were heating up, the whole show stopped as if someone had blown out a lamp.

For some reason, I still have a clear memory of my childish impression of what happened at that moment. I remember people around us, shouting to urge us on. Mama and I were at the height of our victorious revenge when suddenly a tightly braided kamcha[2] snapped across our backs. All three of us screamed and ran. I can't speak for Mama and Munabiya, but I felt as if the skin had been torn off my back and my body had been split in two. I turned and saw that it was my father who had whipped us. Apparently someone had informed him about the leading players in this disgraceful public scene and he had flown out of the room next door where the men were gathered, to bring us back to our senses with his whip.

Pale, his face contorted and his eyes burning with rage,

---

2 Kamcha: whip

he shouted, "A curse on you! A curse!" His thin, bony body trembled. Then he turned his furious eyes on the crowd. The women bleated and fell silent. None of them dared speak.

"Go home, March!" he ordered Mama. Just moments before, Mama had been raging and pulling another woman's hair, but now, afraid of further punishment, she had pushed her way into the back of the room and was hiding behind the other women.

"March!" shouted father. He started towards her, but the women stood shoulder to shoulder, forming a barrier around my mother. It was an impressive display of female solidarity.

Realizing what he was up against, my father had no choice but to leave the room, grinding his teeth.

"He's so quiet you can't get two words out of him, but just look at how he carries that bloody whip!"

"That timid loner's got one hell of a temper!"

"You'd never think it of him!" Feeling bolder, the women let loose a string of snide remarks as Father left. They laughed triumphantly; pleased by the thought that they had got the better of him.

Father was looking to avenge his shame and turned his eyes on the crowd. He wanted a victim on whom he could release his boiling fury. When his irate eyes fell on me, I ducked out of the crowd and raced home.

As I ran, I thought about how people always called Father timid. He was nothing of the sort. When he was angry nothing could stop him, not fear of his own death, and certainly not someone else's. But to be fair, it was rare for him to get this angry.

After a while I stopped running to catch my breath. From there on I walked. I could not stop my tears from flowing, but I was by no means defeated. Up ahead I saw Munabiya. Emboldened by the realization that she could not hear me because I was barefoot, I ran up behind her and pulled her skirt as hard as I could. Then I turned to look at her, as if I had done something particularly worthy. Munabiya had just been publicly whipped by my father, and now she was being burned alive by the shame of it. Her face pale, she staggered along without seeing the path in front of her, dead to the world. I took another look at her and then dashed off when I saw my father approaching us from behind, taking metre-long strides. He still held his whip.

"I bet he'll catch up with Munabiya and give her another one across the back," I thought, and the idea made me turn around again. How would he hit her, and how would Munabiya react? Curiosity stopped me for an instant, but what happened next was not nearly as interesting as what I had expected. Father caught up with Munabiya and, his head bowed, said something to her. Perhaps he was criticizing her, or asking for forgiveness. I did not understand what was happening. Munabiya looked at him sadly; her eyes wide and filled with tears. Then she turned sharply and walked away from him along a narrow path that cut through a field of clover.

I froze, waiting to see what would happen next. Father made a strange motion as if he wanted to go after her, but then he stopped, glanced with annoyance at the people who were staring at him from a distance, and then made straight for me with a threatening look on his face. I took off. When I got home, I hid in a dark corner of the barn and kept an eye on the door, which was partly open. I saw my father stop in the middle of the yard. His face looked terrible, and he grabbed at his shirt where it covered his heart. A second later he broke the wooden handle of his whip, inlaid with silver, over his knee and tossed it into the fire.

Mama did not return straight home, after the scandal,

and Father did not seem to care where she was or what she was doing. He re-lit the fire in his forge, told me to man the bellows as I always did and went right back to work. It wasn't until three days later that all the anger left his face. I saw that he had turned back into the man we all knew, the silent man wrapped up in his secret world. It was our father, Quiet Januzak, a gentle character never prone to outbreaks of rage .

Once things had returned to normal, Mama came back home without announcing her return. First she looked cautiously into the yard, and then she walked with a sure step into her kingdom, muttering something to herself as she picked up scattered woodchips and threw them on the fire. She was not brave enough to pick a fight with Father right away but her eyes showed that her anger was far from forgotten.

Finally, she looked into the workshop and immediately found fault with me. "Just look at you! You look like an abandoned orphan! Get in here and change your shirt and wash yourself!"

That was how she made her masterful entrance to the workshop. After seeing me out, she turned on her husband.

Mama ranted for a long time, releasing all of her pent-up feelings. First she attacked him, then gave a spiteful impersonation of someone She then appeared to excuse her own behavior before finally bursting into spiteful laughter and making fun of Father.

She tried a thousand different ways to provoke a response, but no matter how hard she tried, Father did not move a muscle or say anything to challenge her. He simply kept tapping away with his little hammer. Seeing how indifferent he was to her attacks sent Mama into a real rage. That was when she brought up her chief complaint, the one she only used in very extreme cases when they fought. Although we were too young to understand, we knew that its content was the root of the conflict between them. None of Mama's other complaints ever had the same effect on him.

"I gave you five children, and you don't deserve any of them!" That was her brief preface. "Why can't you find the gold earrings? Where are they? Did you give them to that slut? Come on, tell me!"

As soon as she spoke those words, Father always became furious, sometimes picking up whatever was close at hand and throwing it at her. That was apparently what happened this time. The methodical tapping sound stopped and there was a loud crash. A few seconds later, Mama hastily exited the workshop, rubbing her right shoulder and fixing the scarf that had slipped back on her head.

This marked the end of their exchange of words.

Mama walked around the house making promises to an invisible listener. "I'll get her thrown out of the aul, damn her!" But her voice had lost some of its fight and sounded sad, as if she were acknowledging that this might not happen right away. It could take some time.

That's how anger slowly cools off after a fight. The two parties get pulled back into the daily affairs of this deceptive life and slowly, without noticing it, move ever onwards towards old age, ever closer to the last border somewhere up ahead.

The sight of a familiar junction interrupted my thoughts. I had already reached the place where I needed to turn off to our street. Everything I had been thinking about evaporated as I drove towards our gate and I hastened to put into order, my thoughts and words about why I had come.

I sat nervously inside until I turned off the engine and with it, the car's warm breath. I felt that the unbroken silence was suspicious of me, testing me. Now that Mama was gone, the house seemed less familiar. Perhaps Munabiya was inside.

Perhaps she ran the house now.

I gazed through the windscreen at my father's house, feeling a heavy weight on my heart. No, everything was still the same, from the dark blue window frames, light blue porch and gate, to each and every nail. Somewhere deep inside me, there twinkled a tiny ray of hope that my beloved Mama would come to the gate wearing her usual, brightly printed dress. But no, my most-loved Mama did not appear.

As soon as I got out of the car I heard a hammer tapping in my father's workshop. All of my fears lifted and my heart felt lighter.

The fears that had been gnawing away at me since morning were unfounded. Everything seemed calm; all was in order.

"Hello!" I greeted my father as I entered his workshop. He lifted his head and shook my hand warmly after noticing my guilty, embarrassed face. His lips quivered in a passing smile. As a father, he forgave me and his demeanor seemed to say "Come on in, no-one is angry with you."

Other than this thin smile, we, Januzak's children, rarely saw anything extremely cheerful or angry on his face. Mama was our sole commander. She was the one who punished our misbehaviour. She was the one who spoiled and indulged us. Mama was the only one who went after us with a whip or her fist when necessary.

"Where did you appear from?" asked Father, as he turned back to his work. He raised his hammer but waited to strike. A preconceived idea flashed through my mind; he must be very upset with us to ask a question like that. I looked closely at his face. Something about him had changed. No, he did not look like a man suffering from loneliness or being held under someone's heel. In fact, he looked more like a man who has escaped an illness that had been wearing him down for decades. His face had lost its yellow cast, his eyes were bright and lively, his beard was neatly trimmed and his clothes were clean. He looked well cared-for. Then I noticed the surprise in his eyes. It was obvious that he had not expected me and harbored no grudge against me. For a moment I entertained an absurd notion that I was not even this man's son. Something close to anger touched my heart, but I had no reason to voice this strange sensation. It quickly receded, for I suddenly felt that I was standing next to someone very close to me and I needed his parental love. I found myself loving him as his son. I was overcome by a feeling I had left behind in childhood; he had always been so remote and formal in the way he greeted us, and I wanted him to show that he was glad to see me. I wanted him to put down his hammer and kiss me lovingly on the cheeks. I wanted him to look into my eyes like a loving parent, to examine my hands and follow me around for a while, asking me all sorts of questions about my life. But Father did not notice the change in my soul. He did not see the filial devotion that lit up my face. He retained his aloofness and betrayed no emotion. I realized that I had been unfair in demanding of him the same demonstrative love and unlimited devotion that only mothers are capable of, and I knew that I would never again in my life feel that incomparable, inexhaustible spring of motherly love.

Suddenly, he spoke. "Did you miss the forge? Here, give it a press." My father smiled brightly as if he had finally found the words that were dearest to me.

I took off my coat and began pressing the leather bellows with both hands. I had been away for so long that my hands could not press them evenly and I kept losing my rhythm. Watching me, my father laughed heartily in delight.

"I see you've forgotten," he said, unable to hide his

sincere pleasure and his benign laughter at his grown son's clumsy efforts. I laughed with him at my clumsiness, but more than anything I was affected by my father's joy. His laughter so warmed my soul that I felt tears gathering behind my eyes. The uncomfortable distance between us had disappeared and we began to talk naturally.

"Father, have you been waiting for us to visit?"

"I know how busy you are with your own affairs, son."

"The two years just flew by."

"Two years or two days: It's the same thing."

"I expect it's hard for you being here alone?"

"I'm still alive: Everything's fine, son."

"You can spend this winter in the city. That's what I came to talk to you about."

There was silence.

At first Father pretended that he hadn't heard me, but realizing that he would eventually have to answer, he frowned slightly. I sensed immediately that he did not like the idea.

"I would go," he said in a reserved, almost guilty voice, "but it's impossible, son. If you don't learn to live in the city when you're young, you can't do it once you're old. I couldn't get used to a new way of living."

"Just spend the winter with me. You can come home in the spring. That's what everyone else's parents do."

Father grimaced slightly, as if he had caught a whiff of bad breath on me.

"I don't know who all those people are. They leave the house behind, the animals…"

"But your relatives will keep an eye on the house," I replied, trying not to feel affronted.

Father raised his head and looked hard at me. "So that's really why he's here: to invite me back to the city with him," his eyes spoke eloquently for him.

I patiently waited for a response. Father seemed to be considering what to say.

"Leave me alone," he finally said in a firm voice that did not invite further discussion. "Don't worry about me."

To be honest, I thought I would quickly convince him to return to the city with me. Who wouldn't want to be warm and comfortable in the winter, with plenty of food and a soft bed? But I saw that my father did not share this opinion. Then I decided to describe the advantages of city life, but that made him angry. He was so annoyed that he hit the handle of his hammer on the anvil twice. That hurt my feelings. Father was treating me like a boy who hasn't yet learned to shave. He did not care that I was over forty and beginning to go grey. He had no intention of listening to his grown son or answering me politely. Full of anger and hurt feelings, I began to press the bellows as hard as I could. Under the forge, a column of ashes rose up and dispersed around the room. Father was obviously no longer glad to see me. His whole face was asking, "Why did you come here to bother me?" He turned away from me. Our conversation was over.

While we were busy being upset with each other, the gate creaked open and Adjike-jene, the wife of my father's middle brother, appeared. Stepping into the yard, she immediately began sweeping the front of the porch as if she were at her own home.

"Hello jene," I said, interrupting her work.

"Hello there! Is that you?" she asked in surprise.

I was so glad to see my Adjike-jene that I paid no attention to the obvious point of her question, since she could not have failed to notice my car. I was even happy to accept her kindly chiding, "My God! Why didn't you tell us you were coming?"

Just as Mama had always done, and moving slowly with her characteristic joy, she circled a cup of water above me and then threw out the water to keep sorrows from landing on my head, which was still young by Kyrgyz standards.

Of course, it was thanks to her that my father was so well cared-for: he was well dressed, his face looked good, and he even walked like a young man. I saw that in our absence, baike[3] and jene were not allowing my father to feel lonely. I was filled with gratitude to them.

When we went into the house, that feeling grew. All the rooms shone with cleanliness. The things that had been there during Mama's lifetime were still there, arranged with perhaps even better taste. The potted plants were watered and there was not a speck of dust on the bookshelves. Everything I saw pleased me. It was the kind of home that would lift your spirits.

I wanted to tell Adjike-jene how grateful I was to her for taking care of this old man, but our unwritten rule held me back. Kyrgyz do not thank family members for such care because it is taken for granted that relatives help each other. An expression of gratitude may be interpreted as an empty, wordy accolade that is too easily bestowed. Such praise is only welcome from someone outside the family. Because of this, I just looked respectfully at my jene and felt my love and respect for her grow.

A little later, however, something strange happened between the three of us that ended in a most unexpected and unpleasant way.

It all started when Adjike-jene decided to make tea for us. She wanted to put on the samovar, but she could not find it. After we had finally found the samovar, we realized that

3 Baike : term used to refer to an older male, in this case the father's brother

the matches were gone and the bucket of water was nowhere to be seen. Then we had to find the fire starter. In short, we had to turn everything in the house and the yard upside down.

It was then that I noticed that Mama's cabinets and trunks were not where she had kept them. Instead of helping us as we scrabbled about trying to find things, Father just became more and more miserable. I couldn't understand what was wrong with him. He looked annoyed, jumping up, running around the house and then sitting back down again. He was about to lose his temper. I had never seen him behave like that before and I could not understand why he was angry at jene, the woman who did his washing and cooking.

I kept sending Father looks of surprise and disapproval, but he didn't seem to care. As Adjike rummaged through the house, he made it clear that she was not wanted. I was also a thorn in his side.

My jene took no notice as she opened all the kitchen cupboards, looking for the tea. She could not find it, but she kept looking in every room in the house. I finally realized that she had not been in the house for a long time. The thought of Munabiya came to me. Yes, she must be the one taking care of the house: Or maybe not.

"Where did you put the tea?" I asked jene calmly. Not bothering to answer, she kept rummaging through all the cupboards and shelves. Even more interesting was the fact that she looked every bit as angry as my father did. Her face was red with fury. She kept jerking at her headscarf and mumbling angrily to herself. Her whole face censored my father.

"Thank you for the tea, sister-in-law: That will be enough!" he burst out, no longer able to bear her castigating grumbling. I was shocked to see an elderly man being so rude to a woman, especially his sister-in-law. What had she done? All she wanted to do was make tea for us.

After all that, I expected her to drop everything and go home, but for some reason she did not. Her face did not change in the slightest, as if her brother-in-law's words were not aimed at her, and kept rummaging around to find the tea, all the while muttering terrible things about someone. Father was now green with fury. He was so outraged that I expected him to throw her out.

"I don't want tea. Give me poison! Poison!" he screamed. He was trembling. Again jene gave no reaction, as if my father's wrath wasn't worth a penny to her. That surprised me. What was behind all this? Confused, I had no idea what to say to them or who to stand up for. I wanted to support my jene, but there was something strange in her behaviour. There was some secret between them which was unbeknown to me. Otherwise she would have reacted to his despairing, furious words. She must be guilty of something, but what could it be?

Unable to mediate between them, I decided to stay on the sidelines. More than anything, I was hurt by the realization that my father did not care that I was there. He seemed oblivious to my presence in the room. It did not matter to him that I had come to see him. He was so wrapped up in his own life and his own cares, that he was not ashamed to raise his voice at his sister-in-law. It was unbelievable. Father was responding to her kindness and my filial devotion with black ingratitude.

What was behind it all? Why had my father, whom everyone had always called Quiet Januzak, a man who was restrained and calm by nature, suddenly changed to such an extreme? It was impossible to recognize him in this irrational state. My jaw dropped when he finally lost all control of his temper. He did not know what he was doing: shaking with anger, he jumped up and grabbed the bubbling samovar that jene had just brought in, took it outside and threw it from the porch.

"I won't have any tea! Get together and give me some poison! I need poison!" he shouted hoarsely. Then he went into the other room and slammed the door.

Jene had seen and heard everything her insane brother-in-law had done, but not a muscle in her face moved. She coolly ignored his words.

There was a look of resignation on her face, like a mother patiently waiting for her child's fit of temper to pass.

"What was that performance all about?" I asked her grimly.

She ignored my question. "That's too bad. You need some tea after your trip." It was as if nothing had happened.

"No, tell me what's going on between the two of you. I want an explanation!" I said. I was annoyed that jene paid no attention to me or to anything I said. She looked at me from the corner of her eye with a mixture of surprise and even censure, then said, "Let's go!" and walked out into the yard.

"Nephew, people consider you an intelligent and reasonable man," she began. Her face was white and terrible. "Why are you asking me about your father and his lifestyle here?"

At that moment she looked like a hysterical woman, ready for a fight. I couldn't say anything in response.

"If you're so smart with all your fancy culture, why don't you ever come to visit your father to see how he's doing? Is it because you're still kids, or is it because you don't need your father anymore? You're over forty now, and your youngest brother is thirty. And the three girls, in between, are happy to be supported by their husbands and don't care about anything else. Here, your father has been letting that shameless witch defile your mother's sacred bed. He's been doing things that are so unheard-of and disgraceful that we don't even have words to describe them. I know my poor Shaarkan-jene, bless her memory, is turning in her grave, and not for the first time. Do you know about your mother's last wish?"

I think I stood there like a dunce, just staring at her.

She continued. "When your mother was dying, she said, 'don't ever let that kinless, despised Munabiya cross the threshold of any of the ten sons of Tanai[4]!' Poor Januzak-ake[5] heard her with his own ears, but the she-devil put a spell on him. She has him in her power and never leaves him alone. Can't you see that your father's gone crazy?"

I was saddened by what I heard, but I looked crossly at my jene as soon as a thought occurred to me: "Now I get it. You're the one who wrote that cruel letter." This sudden deduction and the pile of problems that had just landed on my head put me in such a state of confusion that I could not speak. My confusion irritated Adjike-jene, who released even more venom to wound my pride and fire my haltered against Munabiya, the seducer.

"We, the daughters-in-law of Tanai, have become your father's enemies because we are carrying out your dead mother's last wish, but you don't care about any of that. You don't have any honour or pride! Now that you're here, get your father away from that damned witch. Take him back to the city before she drives him crazy. You can see how far it's gone already, can't you?"

Reflecting on all that I had seen, I had to admit that I agreed with her. In her fury, my jene immediately saw that in my face. She moved closer to me and, speaking almost conspiratorially, sometimes even whispering, she began to open my eyes.

---

4 *Tanai : the name of the forefather of the clan*
5 *Ake : used by women when referring to men*

"Get your father away from here!" she said, underlining my chief duty. "Otherwise there's nothing left for us to do. During the day we keep watch and don't let Munabiya near the house. But she waits for nightfall and then slips into your father's bed, damn her! Then as soon as the sun comes up, she creeps away with her tail between her legs. I don't know how she does it. After all, she's already an old woman. Ake is a man, so that's not surprising, but she's nothing but a slut!"

Feeling that she had said too much, she smiled uncomfortably. Then she hissed, "But ake is behaving unworthily. Judging by the way he's acting, he doesn't have a hint of shame."

Jene had been talking to me as if I were a close friend who understood and shared her anxiety, but I found I could not respond rationally. My heart was so dark and heavy that I wanted to get in my car and drive away as quickly as possible, but I couldn't do it.

"Is Akyldbek-baike at home?" I asked. I wanted to discuss my worries with someone else. Otherwise I would have no hope of understanding the relationship between Munabiya and Father that had its roots in the distant past.

"Where else would he be? You know your baike."

The samovar was lying on the ground nearby. She picked it up, found its lid and went back into the house.

While I walked over to Akyldbek-baike's house, I pondered something that had surprised me: every criticism Adjike-jene voiced about Munabiya and every complaint, her manner of expressing her emotions and her entire demeanour, reminded me precisely of my deceased mother. The similarity was striking, as if Mama had willed to this woman everything that had once been hers: her inner life, her feelings, her views of the world and, of course, her jealousy.

I suddenly pictured all of the women of our clan. They were all like Mama regarding one issue. Whenever someone said the name Munabiya, their eyes and mouths became alike.

I think it was only then that I understood how much they all respected my dear Mama for her steadfastness and devotion to family. I also realized that by her decisiveness and determination, Mama stood out from the other women. She made the weather inside her small circle. And because of my father's retiring nature, her word counted for a lot when relatives met to discuss upcoming events, and she took a leading role in making decisions and carrying them out. Perhaps that was why she had such great influence in her family circle, especially with the women. Otherwise there never would have been such difficulties between my father and Adjike-jene over the last wish voiced by poor Mama.

What was I supposed to do with my father if he did not respect Mama's last wish? That was the most difficult decision to make. We living have a sacred duty to respect the last wishes of those who are gone. All the peoples of the earth know that, not just the Kyrgyz. I think it is unforgivable for a person to ignore the last wish spoken by one who is dear. Since ancient times, those who violate that wish are despised for generations. So how was I supposed to react to what my father had done? What would people say? Perhaps the family had already issued a verdict and Adjike-jene was trying to fix the situation somehow? I wanted to know what her husband Akyldbek-baike had to say.

When I entered the room, baike crawled down from his bed before I had a chance to say "salaam alaykum." He had lain down to rest from the continual clicking of his accountant's abacus.

"How is your stomach?" I asked as I made myself

comfortable on the toshok[6]. As always, baike placed his hand cautiously over the place where his stomach ulcer hid and nodded as if to say, "It's alright."

He had worked for the regional government for many years before something broke him. Now he worked in the aul as a simple accountant. There had been a time when he was considered the most educated person in the village, a professional office worker.

Illness had taken hold of him in later years, but whatever the occasion, he never turned down a drink. Helping his ulcer along in this fashion, my baike lost a lot of weight. His suffering from his affliction eventually turned him into skin and bone. He became unfriendly and talked less and less as the years went by. Despite this, he remained on the list of the aul's most respected members.

When I saw the opportunity, I asked about Munabiya.

"Yes, the poor woman lives all alone on the edge of the village. You know that," baike said, looking at me from under his eyebrows. Judging by his calm expression and the sympathy I felt in his reply, she must not be guilty of any of the sins my jene had endlessly described to me. I did not trust his answer for some reason, so I asked him the question that worried me most.

"How should your brother Januzak be punished for ignoring the last wish of the deceased?"

"What last wish?" he asked, looking confused.

"About Munabiya."

"Ah," he said, and smiled with a thousand wrinkles. "I see your dim-witted jene has been whispering to you."

"But is it true what Mama said before she died?" I asked, starting to get worked up.

6 Toshok : a seat on the floor made of animal skins

33

"I don't know. Maybe she did. We were all running around before she died. Maybe Shaarkan-jene said something to her sisters-in-law."

"If it's true what Mama said, then what should we do with Father?"

Without lifting his head, baike gave a strange little laugh. "What should we do? Hang him?"

"We have to say something."

"Say what? Words are just words."

"I don't think so. We all need to speak to him! We should make him respect her last wish!"

"That's very interesting."

"Why do you say that?"

"If your deceased mother was unable to stop him for twenty years, who do think can stop him now?"

I froze. Akyldbek-baike had given up! And the way he had calmly said "twenty years" meant that everyone else was already aware of the situation! Why had none of the family said anything to us, his children? It was strange, and I said as much.

"You were perfectly well aware," said baike without any anger.

"How could we know?" I retorted, my hurt feelings boiling.

"How could you not know? Did you just fall out of the sky? He and your mother fought all the time."

"But we didn't understand…"

"Then you have yourselves to kick. You should have been aware of that kind of thing. Why don't you these understand things like everyone else?"

Baike's face darkened. I felt that the situation would only get worse if the conversation continued. I wanted to avoid further unpleasantness, so I went outside.

"What a mess! A total shambles!" I grumbled to myself. I could not think of an answer to the question posed to me by my grim baike. I was consumed by anger. I had been insulted. I had felt it coming and had subconsciously expected someone to find me at fault for my indifference to my father's spiritual difficulties. Now Akyldbek-baike had done so, coldly and cruelly. His words stung. Why hadn't he found a gentler, more considered way to break the news to me about my father? I could not accept his words and began to protest. Was simple human kindness a shallow luxury between relatives?

I barely made it to my car. Soft near-darkness had already descended on the world. Feeling deeply offended and all too aware of the hopelessness of my situation, I did not know what to do. I reclined the front seats and flopped down on my back. I felt the weight of my conflicted feelings for my father pull at my heartstrings. On the one hand, something urged me to go and tell my father everything he needed to hear, but on the other hand, my heart resisted. It faltered in the face of the "twenty-year story" between two people who were no longer young, at the sheer awareness of those "twenty years," and reflection on the last will of a beloved person who was lost to me. I did not have the strength to do anything about the situation, and my heart was moved to tears by wretchedness. I understood that I, with all my criticism, was nothing but a shadow when compared to what my father was feeling and what he had done. I felt cold and alone. I knew I didn't have the will to say anything to my father. And even if I had, I wouldn't have done so. If he had been my old father, Quiet Januzak, he might have listened to me, who knows? But now he was a stranger to me. He was like a bird that had abandoned its chicks. His emotions and thoughts had left us and flown away to other shores. Akyldbek-baike had sensed it long ago, and that was why he took a nonjudgmental position. He apparently had no choice, at all.

My dear Mama, I'm glad you don't have to see what Father has come to...

My heart ached as I lay in the car.

The emotional tie that had bound Father and Munabiya for so many years did not recognize the duty of the living to the dead, and it shattered an unbreakable, centuries-old spiritual tradition. It seemed to mock both me and Adjike-jene, waving away our just objections, making little of our lofty intention to honour that which was most holy to us : the memory of a person we loved.

What was the solution? Her last wish had to be defended!

If my father did not value his honour, there was no reason to value it for him, but what about the greatest duty that the living have to the dead? What about that duty, Father? I had to ask him that question, whatever the consequences.

With that decision, my heart grew lighter and I moved to get out of the car. Just then, the door of the house opened and my father came outside. In the darkness it was hard to see him. I sat quietly in the car, wondering if he would look for me. He went out of the gate and walked silently past me. He did not pause at the car. I immediately knew that he was not going to his brother Akyldbek's house. I wanted to follow him, but he might have heard me if I had opened the car door, so I had to stay there and watch his silhouette through the glass. I was right: he was going to Munabiya. Perhaps it's better that way, I thought to myself.

Before he had gone far, Father ran into someone. I heard a woman's voice. Father seemed to be inviting her back into the house, but she refused. She must have seen my car. All of a sudden, Adjike-jene leapt out as if in ambush and began berating the one she despised.

"Did you see that, kichine bala[7]? I told you! She never leaves us in peace, even at night! Where are your shame and conscience, Munabiya? Shouldn't you be ashamed of yourself, in front of this boy?"

I jumped out of the car and grabbed jene by the arm. Even while I was trying to shut her up, she managed to spit out a dozen more words of scorn. Munabiya walked quickly away, and my father approached us, silently. I was afraid that the fight from earlier on would start again. After seeing him throw the boiling samovar, I knew that Father's nerves were stretched to the limit. He had become unpredictable. Adjike-jene had no intention of leaving; in fact, she pushed her way into our yard.

"Jene, go home!" I grabbed her by the elbow. That seemed to surprise her. She was not afraid of my father in the least, and obviously did not feel even the most basic respect for him.

Father had obviously calmed down after I'd left him. He now came to me with a white bundle under his arm and asked if I would spend the night. When I agreed, he went inside and turned on the light, utterly ignoring jene, who stood close beside me.

When she and I went inside, Father opened the bundle. He showed me the washed and ironed towels and tablecloth and said, "Look, I asked your jene to wash these things two weeks ago and she did so, but I cannot have a conversation with her." I looked at Adjike. His words had no more impact than if he'd said nothing. She was busily putting the samovar that he had thrown outside back on the fire to heat.

We ate a dinner of sorts and she left, after which Father

---

7 Kichine bala : term used by a woman when speaking to her husband's younger brother.

began to make his own bed.

When an old man ,left alone without the care of a woman, tries to make his own bed and can't work out which is the inside and which is the outside of the blanket cover, it makes for a pitiful scene, especially in a Kyrgyz aul.

"Go to bed," instructed Father, pointing to the living room. I saw that he had no desire to talk to me. All the words I had prepared might be left unspoken. I had to start the conversation somehow.

"Father, what was Mama's last wish?"

"Why do you ask?"

"I just want to hear it."

Father turned his face to the wall, pulled the blanket up to his chin and made a point of making himself comfortable. Then he lay still for a minute, without saying anything. Finally he gave voice to his displeasure.

"She said a lot of things, poor woman... She told us to lay her on the big, bright rug that used to hang in the living room and cover her with brocade cloth. 'Do not give people the devil's vodka until my body touches the bottom of the grave. Have my children and my husband, leaning on his stick, mourn me for forty days, and have my sisters-in-law , leaning on their sticks, mourn me for seven days, and have my sisters-in-law continue their koshoki[8] for seven days.' That's what she said."

My heart contracted. I remembered how I had been in a big hurry to get back to work three days after my mother's funeral. Mama surprised me. My poor Mama: why had she said all those things?

But of course, no one passes judgment on the last wishes of the dying.

"Father," I said and went to the head of his bed, "why

8 Koshoki : funerary poems for the dead

38

didn't you keep us here for seven days if that's what our mother wanted?"

He looked hard at me. "Would you have stayed?"

"We should have stayed."

"Would your bosses have let you stay?"

"We could have taken time off."

"If everyone spent seven or eight days burying their dead, who would be left to do any work?"

"That's not your problem."

"Go to bed!"

"What did Mama say about Munabiya?"

"I didn't hear."

"How could you not hear? People are talking about it!"

"Nobody's talking. Go to bed."

"Don't try to evade the issue. We have to talk!"

"Turn off the light."

I did not turn the light off and remained where I was. I stood there for a long time without moving. I thought he would eventually answer me, but my father stubbornly said nothing. Determined to get his attention, I sniffed and coughed loudly. Eventually, Father slowly rolled over, sat up heavily and looked at me with something like anguish in his eyes.

"Was it the purpose of your visit to open up an investigation against me?" he asked wearily. His head flinched nervously. "Everybody else has already seen fit to mock me and now it's your turn, right? Would it make you happy if I upped and died?"

"We're talking about Mama's last wish," I said, concealing the effect his question had on me.

"Your mother never said anything that concerned Munabiya. It's all lies made up by your Adjike-jene!"

When he began, he was yelling so loudly that his voice

was hoarse, but by the end he was quiet, on the verge of tears. I felt sorry for him, but my filial feelings for my deceased mother outweighed any pity I felt for my father.

"Maybe she didn't, but Adjike-jene says that was what she wanted. You have to obey that!" I adopted a tone that forbade any disagreement.

Father looked up at me, his eyes damp with tears. His face was twisted with indescribable grief.

"Then I'd be better off dead. Fools like you aren't capable of understanding the desires of a living man. I don't have any choice but to die."

I realized, too late, the message conveyed in his tired, grief-stricken eyes.

Had I failed to understand what he was trying to express to me at that moment? No, quite the opposite. I foolishly enjoyed seeing my father bow his grey head, unable to say a word in his own defense. I felt like I had won. The next day I hurried back to the city. I remember that I was in a fairly good mood, feeling like I had at least done my duty.

Three days later, all of his children, received a telegram. By the time we got back to the aul, the yurta[9] was already up and my poor father lay in it, asleep for eternity. The only evidence of his last fleeting moments of life on this earth was the toshok spread upon the now cold, wet clover on the frozen ground of late autumn. A thin, worn grass mat and a silk curtain hid my father from us, the mourning members of his family.

I regained my composure once my tears had released the sorrow of loss. While I was talking with the relatives and friends who had come to share our grief, and especially with the aksakals[10], I sensed that someone very close to my father

9 Yurta : at funerals, the Kyrgyz place the deceased in a white tent called a yurta
10 Aksakal : the senior male member of the clan

was missing; someone had not come to mourn him. Later on I realized that person was Munabiya. Listening to quiet discussions in the family, I noticed that Adjike-jene led all of Mama's sisters-in-law in a categorical refusal to allow her to be present.

The male half of the family, on the other hand, seemed to be suggesting that Munabiya ought to be formally invited if she were not brave enough to come on her own accord. Those were the two opposing views. I was preoccupied with the loss of my father and had no desire to take part in the discussion. She could come or stay away as she pleased: I did not care, and felt that her presence would not change anything. But if Adjike-kene and the other women were against it, then I saw no reason to contravene and reignite the conflict by inviting her.

At that point, a man came over and said that Konokbai-aksakal wanted to see me. I followed him towards the elder of the village, who was sitting nearby.

He greeted me with sympathy and friendship. "Come here, son. Come and sit down. Have you released your sorrow by tears? Is your heart lighter? The way you mourn for your father is the way your own children will mourn for you," Konokbai-aksakal patted my hand. He then broached the reason he wanted to see me.

"My dear Taken, there is no life without complications and loss. We all share the same fate. Life is not always easy, but it is also not always hopeless and hard. We consider you to be a fairly intelligent and reasonable man. That is why we have invited you to our council. Before he died, your father desired one thing. We cannot fail to do as he wished."

I sat in silence with my head bowed, listening to the respected aksakal.

He continued. "Your father said, 'Let Munabiya sit by my

body at my head. Let her wear mourning clothes and weep for me.'"

Everything went dark in my eyes. It was a terrible blow for me to hear my poor father's last wish.

That last look he had given me, that look of hate and suffering in his moist eyes, now entered my heart like an arrow and I lost all of my strength.

I could not move, much less speak, and I remained sitting in front of Konokbai-aksakal with my head bowed low.

Konokbai- aksakal called to a boy nearby, "Hey lazybones, come here! Run over to Munabiya's house and tell her that Januzak-ata wanted her to come and mourn him. Got it? Just say that and nothing else. She'll make up her own mind."

I understood that, for decency's sake, Konokbai needed to inform me of their decision to invite Munabiya. They did not need my permission.

The members of the clan of Tanai and all of the friends who had come to see Father off on his last journey, each dressed in mourning clothes, waited in anticipation. Some of them kept their curiosity more or less hidden, but with others it was obvious. Everyone wanted to know whether or not Munabiya would appear. And if she came, how would she look?

Time stood still.

Adjike-jene caught wind of the fact that an invitation had gone out to Munabiya. She immediately stopped her weeping, ducked out of the yurta and grim faced, subjected Konokbai-aksakal to a torrent of disrespectful verbal abuse. She was not afraid of him and gave no weight to his authority.

"What's this I hear? Why are you, a respected man, ordering such a disgraceful thing?!" Full of righteous wrath, she turned to the crowd. "If he's so just and fair, then why didn't he try to enforce Sharrkan-jene's dying wish? A woman's will doesn't mean anything, does it? Just look at the likes of him! They always do whatever they want!"

One of the men tried to reason with her. "Listen, Adjike! You fulfilled your jene's dying wish. Did you let Munabiya cross Janauzak's threshold while he was alive? You didn't! So why won't you let Munabiya do her duty to see him off now that he's dead?"

Adjike-jene leapt over to the man and, as if she had just caught sight of her mortal enemy, screamed hysterically in his face, "Munabiya will not come here! What right does she have to mourn at the coffin of another woman's husband? If all the men in the clan of Tanai have lost their honour and dignity and insist that Munabiya come, then let them run down to her house in a big group! You can all go and live with her, under her skirt!"

Some of my relatives began to snigger, but others were clearly displeased by Adjike-jene. They winced and turned away from her. Still, there were some who continued to watch her in amusement.

Adjike cast another look of outrage at everyone and went back into the yurta.

No one said a word against her, and that indicated that Adjike-jene now occupied the post of leader among the women in the clan, as my mother had once been. She demanded unquestioned authority and influence.

There were too many people at the funeral to fit into the yard, so small groups gathered outside the gate and along the street. Many were sitting like a flock of black jackdaws on rows of benches, brought out for the occasion.

According to tradition, as the men arrived they went first to the yurta and, hands at their belts, hung their heads and wept together for the deceased. The women in the yurta answered them in unison, harmonizing their koshoki. Suddenly the young women who were running around the yard with teapots and dishes began whispering in agitation and pointing at the road.

"She's coming," the whispers abounded. Anticipating Munabiya's arrival, people stopped talking, lifted their heads and froze in open curiosity. Everyone who was watching had their own reasons for being interested in Munabiya's arrival. For some, it was honour. For others, it was shame. Yet others welcomed the opportunity to sneer. Some simply wanted a chance to laugh, and then there were those who were curious and nothing more.

I was embarrassed and overcome by contradictory emotions. However more than anything , I was worried that the women would cause a scandal.

Suddenly, in the absolute, breathless silence, fluffy white snowflakes began to fall from the pale, milky sky. Thicker and thicker they fell, racing each other as they made their way to the ground. They were racing to cover the grey, bereaved world with a blanket of white. The air became crisp and clear and people could breathe more easily. There was a feeling of freshness, of cleanliness in mind and body, as if you had rinsed your entire being in the morning dew.

Munabiya walked proudly up the middle of the street, all alone. Her long black shawl covered her head, which was bowed slightly to one side, and cascaded over her dark clothes.

The curious crowd split in two, creating a path for Munabiya up to the yurta. When she reached the edge of the crowd, she lowered her head further, gathered the edges of her shawl to her chest, and began to weep out loud. We could see that she had been mourning my father quietly on her own since the previous day. Her face was washed with tears and slightly puffy. Tears flowed freely like a spring from her red eyes.

Several young men standing by the yurta bowed their heads and began to mourn in response to Munabiya[11]. As was fitting, the women in the yurta began to weep again. However, soon the crying broke off. Adjike-jene had stopped them. When she realized that Munabiya was there, she ran out of the yurta, her eyes, thunderous. I took a step forward, worried at what might happen.

Munabiya had stopped crying. Her tear-filled eyes shone as she walked straight toward Adjike-jene, who stood bravely with her hands in fists, as if meeting an attacker head-on. Her plump body trembled like a green leaf in a strong wind. It seemed that something incredible was about to happen. Either Munabiya would stop, or jene would have to let her pass. The women did neither, and soon were standing almost face to face.

Just at the decisive instant, one of the aksakals broke the electric silence. "Somebody tell that stupid woman to let this person past! You can't block someone who has come to mourn the deceased!"

While the aksakal was venting his annoyance, Akylbek-baike managed to squeeze through the crowd. He grabbed his wife by the arm and pulled her to one side. Adjike-jene did not want to obey her husband. She broke away from him and pushed her way back to Munabiya. When Munabiya turned to look at her, her eyes seemed to burn the other woman with the power of her sorrows. That was when something snapped inside my jene. She lost her nerve. Something within her broke, and the fire in her eyes went out. Seeing that, I felt calmer. A brief thought passed through my mind: "It would be a good thing if she was always that docile." Her fury, however, was not gone. It was just momentarily hidden. As soon as Munabiya entered the yurta, Adjike-jene came back to life. She pinched

---

11 By tradition, men and women take turns mourning in a "call and response" fashion

her cheek as if she wanted to rip a piece out of it.

"Shameless hussy!" she screamed, looking mainly at the other women. "She's wearing the gold earrings that Januzak-ake lost all those years ago!" She looked to the crowd, hoping for support, but found none in the people's faces.

I immediately recalled how my parents had fought when the gold earrings my father had made went missing. I had heard hints, started and enlivened by Mama that they had been taken by "that thief Munabiya."

Several women, under my mother's leadership, had even organized a party to search the poor, solitary woman's house.

It appeared that Adjike-jene had not forgotten the valuable earrings. Now she wanted to resurrect the old slander, born out of jealousy and burning hate, and pour it onto Munabiya.

"How horrible," I thought to myself.

The squabbling was constant. Naïve but by no means innocent, my poor Mama had demanded that Father find the missing earrings, up until the very day she died. It was her means of letting off steam whenever jealousy overpowered her. I remember Father tolerating all of her assaults on him except when she mentioned those earrings. People said they represented the best work my father had ever done in his whole life.

The women in the yurta resumed their koshok honouring the deceased. They expressed the hope that his soul would live in paradise. They reminded us of the great loss to his children, friends and all the people living in this deceitful world.

At first it was hard to pick out Munabiya's voice from the sound of the other women singing, but suddenly one particularly sorrowful voice rang out above the rest. I have never heard anything like it, before or since. The voice grew more powerful, like the rushing of high water in the spring. It overflowed with bitter regret. The voice expressed a special kind of suffering, and it sang strange words that were not ones usually used by women during mourning. Munabiya was releasing all her sorrow in a torrent of tears and reconciling her terrible loss. Everyone around the yurta and in the yard felt it. We all strained to hear the lone tragic voice. I took a stool and sat by the yurta so that I could focus on listening to her. With each word she sang, my head sank lower. I closed my eyes to hold back the hot wave of tears that rose from the depths of my heart.

The song was her farewell, but it also contained a tiny ray of hope for her beloved.

We lost our way
When we came into this world,
Januzak.
Our life on earth did not know
Joy and feasting, Januzak.
Caught in our silent
Joyless fate, Januzak,
My light has gone out.
I am tired of this hard path, Januzak.
If you find peace
In the dark earth, Januzak,
What shall keep me here?
I will go after you, Januzak.
If you are not in the earth,
If you go to the skies, Januzak.
I will go there, too,
Sooner or later. Wait for me, Januzak.
There was no kindess or bliss
For us in this world, Januzak.
Scorn and loathing
Were my fate, Januzak.

You have gone to your eternal home,
My dear Januzak.
That is the only place we can be together
In love, Januzak.

Through a veil of tears I saw people standing perfectly still, covered from head to foot in soft, white snow, as they listened to that lonely, sorrowful song. The whole world was white: the people, the earth, the yurta, the trees and sky. Everything froze in sorrowful silence. It seemed as if the whole world had changed because of the breathtaking weeping of a woman in love. The other women standing and sitting nearby changed in front of my eyes. Their faces were no longer unkind. At that moment, I sensed that their thoughts and feelings united with the soul of that one devoted, loving woman.

I saw that something had touched the strings of the women's hearts. In that moment, they came together as one in their realization of their greatness compared to us men, of their ability to remain true to their love until the very end.

Touched by Munabiya's sorrow, the women's faces revealed what was understood: a woman honours the man she loves, both in life and after he leaves this world.

The aksakals and all of the men had been talking until Munabiya began her mourning, but now they sat hunched and strangely silent. Then Munabiya came out of the yurta.

The wide edges of her black shawl thrown over her shoulders did little to hide her lithe figure. She was still beautiful. For an instant she looked in my direction, but she did not see me. She glanced at the aksakals, but she didn't seem to see them, either. She looked around in surprise at the transformed world, and then dropped her eyes to the white earth. The crowd was silent as she stepped into the pure, untouched snow and walked away.

The silence was rudely broken when some boys and girls playing nearby began to laugh. No one expected the laughter, and everyone was shocked.

One of the aksakals brushed the snow from his sleeve and grumbled, "Drat those kids." The children found his displeasure ridiculous and laughed again. Then they all joined hands and ran off.

An old woman smiled with pleasure. "Just look at the little kittens. They've found each other and are holding hands." She beamed at the children's backs as they ran away.

Munabiya was gone.

Konokbai raised his voice. "Hey! Boy! Go after Munabiya and tell her to come back. Tell her to see Januzak off on his voyage." He was talking more to the people around him than the boy.

The boy caught up with Munabiya. She stopped to stroke his hair and then went on without a word.

To this day, I do not know why Munabiya did not listen to the aksakals and come back.

I would ask her, but she is no longer with us …

May you never be forgotten, my blessed mother Munabiya!

Perhaps your soul has found eternal peace and love.

SHAHIDKA

From the Author

Brief – very brief – is the lifetime of feelings in the human soul. But there remain certain impressions, perhaps from long ago, that even death cannot erase. When that happens, it is natural to wonder if they might contain a lesson for you or for someone else. After all, there must be a reason for that feeling, that impression, to live on in your soul. It has its reason for living and nothing you can do will stop it. Perhaps you'll forget about it for a while , but it lies warming like a coal hiding in the ashes ready to leap back into flame when you least expect it. Perhaps the feeling that has been with you during your whole life will actually outlive you. The body is of this earth, but what about thought? Has anyone ever seen or touched thoughts and feelings? People give birth to thoughts and then they die, but their thoughts live on and prosper, independent of the mortals who created them.

Those are the thoughts that fill my soul today.

I have already walked the greater part of the path measured out to me by the Creator. Over the years I have created a great world within me ;a secret world behind seven seals, a world that, to be honest, I have yet to fully understand.

So I dare to believe that this narrative may be an enduring lesson for some and an entertaining story for others.

It happened when I was about thirty, trying without much success to find a wife, my chances slipping away with each passing year. It was not a routine, everyday occurrence, but rather, a strange incident that took place in Balykchy on the western shore of Issyk-Kul. The city obstinately survives the wild winds that assault it, and its people have inherited its stubbornness and determination.

It was winter. Although the forecasters probably knew, they felt no need to explain where the wild wind, the Ulan, came from and why it tried to blow the water out of Issyk-Kul to the east. When the Ulan raises white-capped waves and rakes over the lake, turning it inside out, the deep groan that seems to come from the very bottom of Issyk-Kul reaches all the way to the ear of our Creator. On those days, people say that the mountain known as Kyzyl-Ompol is in a rage. Bending against the onslaught of the wind, they pull their fur hats down to their eyes and tie them tighter under their chins. Little do they know that the cliffs of Kyzyl-Ompol have nothing to do with it. The fault lies in the Boom Gorge.

In ancient times, the river Jan-Daira broke out of Lake Issyk-Kul and dug the Boom Gorge, which to this day forms a natural pipe connecting the Chu Valley with the Issyk-Kul Valley. While the lake retains the summer's warmth all winter, the Chu Valley becomes bitterly cold and the difference in air pressure pushes cold air through the pipe of the Boom Valley. When the wind breaks out of the valley, it becomes the Ulan, the hurricane.

It was on a winter evening, with the bone-chilling Ulan howling through the streets, that a wedding party took place at a restaurant in town. At the "king's table," where the bride and groom were sitting, a fight suddenly broke out. The shocked guests leapt to their feet. No one could figure out what happened, and no one knew what to do. In an instant the scuffling escalated into a real brawl. The two sides turned the restaurant into a battlefield, as if there had been advance preparation. Cups, spoons, plates and chairs went flying. Just then I remembered the bride! Svetlana Cherkashina had been sitting at the top table in her snow-white veil just moments before, but now she was gone. The groom, Sergei Samsonov, who was an Alexander Nevsky look-alive, was embroiled in the middle of the fight and covered from head to foot in blood.

Sergei was as tall as a poplar and exuded the might of a true Russian warrior. Nevsky had nothing on him. I had my reasons for disliking him, but I'll give him this: he may not have been Svetlana's equal, but he didn't fall short by much. Svetlana was a real Russian beauty. I say that as a statement of fact, not because I loved her. She was more than beautiful. She was magnetic and radiated an inner light. A fairytale princess with the moon in her hair and a star on her brow: that was Svetlana. Whenever she walked into one of the dim offices of our flour mill, she cast a magical light on everything around her. She could have behaved like a princess, but she didn't. She had a decisive, masculine turn of mind and was as impulsive as a flying arrow. She solved the most complex of problems as though they were games. As her manager, I sometimes felt annoyed that I couldn't solve these problems on my own and I envied her for her skills and her talented leadership. God had been generous to her, giving her a fine face, body and mind. Fate, however, tends to deal a different hand.

Svetlana shouldn't have invited me to her wedding. And I shouldn't have told her that I loved her more than life itself. Even though Sveta had told me she could hardly wait for her fiancé to get out of the army, I asked her father for her hand in marriage. I did it because she never actually told me "no." She just kept postponing things, sometimes turning my feelings into a joke, sometimes appearing to believe me. Oh, the moonlit and moonless nights we spent pressed against each other! I belonged to her, body and soul, and I hoped to find my happiness with this wonderful girl.

But then one fine morning she fluttered into my office, cheerful as always, and put a wedding invitation on my desk. It was as if there had never been anything between us. There was a photograph on the invitation: a picture of she and her classmate Serge, leaning against each other like a pair of doves.

Even though I was consumed by suspicion that things might turn out this way, the actual evidence caught me unaware. My heart gave a lurch and blood rushed to my face. I was probably blushing to my ears. I don't remember how I managed to hold my nerve. But what could I do? She had told me more than once that she already had someone. I frantically tried to put something like a smile on my face.

"I appreciate the invitation, but I'm afraid I'd feel out of place at your wedding."

Sveta seemed oblivious to the fact that I felt like she was cutting my guts open with a blunt knife. "The boss is always an honoured guest. It won't be a wedding if you don't come." She pressed my hand and vanished through the door.

She became a stranger to me in that instant, but the delightful vision that had captured my mind and soul still lingered in the office. I could have picked a fight with her, but my heart didn't dare. There was a hurricane in my chest! The third wheel! There had always been an incoherent awareness, buried deeply in my mind that the phrase applied to me but hope, everlasting hope, had pulled me along. How hard it is to extinguish the flames of hope once it catches fire!

Svetlana had accepted my stubborn attraction to her. She hadn't stopped me from courting her. But she had also never hidden the fact that her heart would always belong to Sergei. In denial, I had assumed she was testing the strength of my passion. I had driven myself wild and gone to extremes to prove my love to her, but it turned out that testing me was the furthest thing from Sveta's mind. She just spoke honestly and openly. The proof was on my desk: The wedding invitation. Like a bullet to the head!

The rest of the day was a mess. I was preoccupied by one thought: should I go to the wedding or not? At noon some employees came by to ask me for money so that they could give the newlyweds a wax bear surrounded by wax bear cubs.

I think that everyone at the company was well aware of how I felt about Sveta. I was a terrible conspirator and had been the target of teasing and even ire from some of the girls. It took me too long to realize that an unmarried boss makes a perfect subject for gossip. I was thirty years old and had yet to find my other half. There had already been many girls in my life, and I suppose my parents eventually just gave up. The last time she mentioned it, my mother said that they were tired of nagging and I was welcome to live how I pleased. She hasn't said a word since. I am trying to start a family but it just hasn't worked out! I swear I've been trying!

On that day, the hope I had nurtured in my heart left me. I would go to the wedding, not my own wedding, but someone else's, and as a guest, not the groom. Not going wasn't an option. What kind of boss would I be if I wasn't prepared to share my employees' moments of joy and shoulder the burden of their sorrows? I don't know how other people live, but that's how we Kyrgyz feel. If I didn't go, my employees' solidarity would suffer. They would be disappointed. I didn't need that.

What could I do? My biggest concern was to prevent people at work from entertaining suspicions and that is how I talked myself into accepting Sveta's invitation.

* * *

Nobody knew for sure what instigated the trouble at the wedding. As soon as the scuffle started sending dishes and chairs flying, the guests began to make a beeline for the door outside. All I remember is that the fight started somewhere near to the table where the bride and groom were sitting. The first cups and spoons flew from that direction. Some of the food landed on me. Instantly more people got involved in the fight, and the hall turned into a bloody battlefield. Both sides were fighting to the death. I went for the door, but chaos had already turned into a maelstrom and I could only feel my way through the room with my arms covering my head in protection.

Sveta was nowhere to be seen. That was surprising. As I tried to escape I realized that this fight could ruin her chances of ever being happy. No matter who was at fault, it would be a black stain on her fate. It even occurred to me that she might try to kill herself. I hit a couple of people in the ribs with a chair to get to the door, but the exit was blocked by fighting bodies and I found myself face to face with a solid barrier: the restaurant bouncer.

"Where's the bride? Where is she?" I yelled. He shrugged, jerked his head toward the kitchen and disappeared. His gesture felt somewhat reassuring. Apparently Sveta was hiding out with the cooks: good thinking on her part.

Just then the outside door gave way with a crack and fell into the street. A tangle of bodies tumbled through the doorway, but the police were already blocking the escape route with their nightsticks.

Someone shouted, "The fighting's in there. Go and arrest them. We're just guests."

The police quickly sized up the situation and began letting people out one by one. I managed to get to my car and locked myself in. Outside the windows, the Ulan was blowing a mixture of sand and snow. It was bitterly cold. Meanwhile, three of my employees ran over and joined me in the car. Two of them were women. The third was my broker, Sapar. He'd got the worst of it and his face was beaten up.

I asked them if they had seen Sveta. One of the women said that Sveta had run off toward the kitchen.

"How horrible: I've never heard of anything like this!"

"Idiots! No sooner do we sit down to dinner than they're already drunk!"

"What a nightmare!"

"It's Sveta and Sergei's fault for inviting those kinds of people."

"What are you talking about? It was Sergei who started the whole thing."

"The fighting?"

"You bet!"

"No way. That wouldn't have happened."

And yet, I couldn't help asking. "How did Sergei start it?"

"His brother Viktor was sitting next to him, and Sergei threw a dish in his face."

"Just like that?"

"They'd been arguing about something."

"Was Sergei drunk?"

"He kept leaving the room, but he didn't touch the champagne in front of him."

"Morons like that don't drink champagne. He was

probably shooting up. I was watching him."

"How terrible! It's just terrible!"

"Sveta didn't know he'd got hooked on drugs in the army."

"She probably thought she could fix him."

"You can't fix that kind."

"It's love! Sveta may be pushy, but she loved him blindly like a little girl."

"Poor kid. That's tough luck."

"I'd call it a terrible tragedy!"

Sapar put a word in. "The strange thing is that Sveta's family and all of her brothers weren't fighting on Sergei's side. They were on Viktor's side. For the life of me I can't figure out why."

The women started laughing.

"So you got hit for taking Sveta's family's side."

"I was trying to stop them, I swear."

"And you got what you deserved. Stick your nose in and it gets knocked off. You'll know next time."

I burst out, "Why were they on Viktor's side? And why did Sergei hit him? Why did Sergei hit his brother?"

"Who knows, boss. They're all related and live across the street from each other. There's always been some kind of feud between them. They pull knives on each other all the time. Everyone knows that."

One of the women turned to the other, "You said that they were going to marry her off to Viktor instead of Sergei. Is that true?"

"I told you what I heard. It's true."

At that point I lost it. "Did you say she was supposed to marry Viktor?"

"Viktor was dating Sveta; In secret."

"Sergei's own brother?" I was practically shouting.

"Right. I think that's what the fight was about."

I don't remember how I jumped out of the car. It took hurricane-force winds blowing snow in my face to cool me off. By then the police were shoving a bunch of handcuffed fighters into their van. I thought I saw both Sergei and his brother Viktor among them. I raised my collar to protect my cheeks, but my hands completely froze while I watched the scene. I was involuntarily still looking for Svetlana. Where was she? Where had she disappeared to? I had some harsh things to say to her. My blood was boiling. What kind of girl was she? How could she date two brothers at the same time?

One of my employees wound down the car window. "Boss, don't stand there without a hat. Get back in the car," she called.

But I ... I ran through the whirling snow toward the restaurant. The only people left inside were policemen in red caps, with a few guests huddled in groups. The police eyed them and from time to time, worked over the louder ones. Two or three drunken guests kept yelling.

One of them was saying, "That groom, I'm gonna kill him. I'll kill the bastard! Remember my words! I'll kill him!"

I looked closer. Was it Viktor? It wasn't. Why did some random drunk man want to kill Sergei? What had he ever done to him? Was he another boyfriend of Sveta's? Nothing made sense. My head was spinning.

Just then I caught sight of a police major with a moustache. Assuming he was in charge, I ran over to him.

"Have you found the bride?" I asked, out of breath.

"What?"

"You have to find the bride!"

"Who the hell are you? Get out of here!" the Major

shoved me in the chest. Enraged, I went for him, but I caught a nightstick between my shoulder blades. I saw sparks as if they'd hit me with a hot metal rod and went down like a fallen tree.

The major waved at the others. "Put him in the van!"

That's how I found myself packed into a black police van with a crowd of drunken rowdies.

* * *

In the middle of the night, the steel door to the stinking room, or so-called infirmary, where they had unloaded us creaked open. A light was switched on and an unfamiliar captain started bawling at us.

"Svetlana Cherkashina is missing. The police are looking for her. Which of you are going to volunteer to help find her?"

Everyone had been dead asleep and snoring, but from all corners I could hear voices mumbling "Me. I'll go." I too spoke up. The captain pointed to me first. I hadn't been asleep. I was too angry: Angry at Svetlana. That night I had searched this mob for Viktor and Sergei, but they weren't with us. I guessed they were locked up elsewhere.

The captain chose three of us. They took us straight to the Cherkashins' house. Inside we found Sveta's mother and father, bent over and wiping away the tears that came to their eyes. Her father, Danil Grigorievich, a carpenter, knew me well. I had always shown him respect, as you would your future father-in-law.

Seeing me, he came forward and exclaimed: "My daughter's missing!"

"We'll find her, Danil Grigorievich," I promised, trying to comfort him.

In fact, I had no idea where to look for Sveta. Soon the fussy, moustached Major from the previous night appeared and told us where we would be looking.

"First things first: We'll check the shores of the lake. Dry land can wait!"

* * *

The wind was particularly harsh at the shore; something we had all known since childhood. By the lake a person becomes doubly obstinate and twice as tough. That's because the three elements – earth, water and sky – show their strength and the power of their confrontation most keenly at the point where they converge. The fury of the waves and the vehemence of the wind, that boiling epitome of nature, harden the human soul.

The Major chewed on his words and swallowed them as he tried, inarticulately, to explain the search strategy to us. They divided the men into two groups. My group was sent to a fairly deserted part of the beach, a narrow strip of shore almost completely overgrown with bushes that ran down to the lake's edge. We were given powerful torches and were to look for footprints in the sand. When the high waves receded, exposing several metres of beach uncovered by vegetation, we ran out to look there too. A sergeant with a dog raced ahead of us.

After hours of determined but futile searching, both parties regrouped on a high point on the shore. We could barely drag our legs. Sand filled our ears, noses, mouths, eyes and even our clothes. The wind pounded our backs, as if it wanted to get rid of us.

"We can't search the lake. Those waves won't let you get near the water."

"If you go looking for death, you're sure to find it."

"Trouble always takes you by surprise."

"Svetlana wasn't the kind of person to take her own life. This is a load of nonsense."

"She was mad and ran off. Now I bet she's hiding out with friends."

"What happened to her wouldn't be easy for anyone."

I listened to scraps of conversation carried by the wind but said nothing. I agreed with one opinion at least: No matter how terrible her wedding had turned out, Sveta would never commit suicide. As far as I could tell, she had been far from obsessed with the idea of getting married and having children. On the contrary, she had other, more important and far-reaching plans.

* * *

There were times when Svetlana got carried away with romantic fantasies that I could not understand. There was a period when she used the word "levitation" in every other sentence.

"What's that?" I asked.

She answered, "I want to rise up in the sky and fly. Sometimes I have so much energy and strength inside my chest that I feel I'll burst. They just boil over and I start burning like a flame. Like a fire. And I want to shoot up into the sky like a bullet and fly way up in the clouds."

"If you're up there in the clouds, who is going to sell our bags of flour and bran?"
I thought joking would bring her down to Earth but it didn't. I suppose she felt I'd muddied all of the bright dreams that sprang from her young soul, like a fountain reaching for the sky. She turned around and left.

On another occasion, she casually commented, "I think I was a crane in a previous life."

"What did you say?" I didn't get it.

"A crane," she repeated. "Cranes are the most wonderful birds. They fly around the whole world as free as can be. Cranes stretch out their necks and fly so perfectly and so high. Whenever I see them, my soul tries to break out of my chest because it wants to be free! I want to go with them, but I can only stand there and watch them until they disappear. Then the tears come..."

"Maybe," I replied, not wanting to hurt her feelings again, "maybe you really were a crane."

Sveta suddenly turned to me. "What about you?"

"Me? I guess I was a miller. Like now." I didn't know how to do anything else. That was all that came into my head, so I said it. She must have thought I was joking, for she laughed heartily.

"That means you have to try to be the best, the most honest miller in this lifetime. You have to be an example for all the other millers in the world. That's the whole point of reincarnation."

"Are you saying I'm a bad miller?"

"Average. We'll come back another two or three times and see how you're doing."

"Okay. But I want us to be together always, no matter what world we're in."

Sveta laughed. "But I might be a crane in my next life."

Then I remembered something else. Lots of memories come to you at a time like that.

It was a summer day. Sveta and I were out on the lake on a catamaran and out of the blue she asked me if I was afraid of death. Maybe the question came from looking into the ink-black depths of the lake.

"Sure," I answered, eyeing the deep. "Everyone's afraid of death."

"It's fine to be afraid of dying accidentally. But why be afraid of an honest death?" Her voice was contemplative.

I looked at her curiously. "Give me an example."

Sveta laughed. Her voice was clear. "Here's an example. If you were drowning, I'd jump in after you without even thinking about how I might perish."

"Oh, I see!" I exclaimed and took her by the shoulders. "Well, now I won't fear death. Not when you're around."

"That's not what I meant. I can see you're still afraid."

I was piqued. "How can you see that?"

"It's not obvious. Don't worry. But I can read your thoughts in your face."

"Is that what you call physiognomy?"

Sveta nodded. Then she dived from the catamaran into the deep.

* * *

No, with thoughts and ideas like those, Svetlana didn't seem like the kind of person who would end her life over a drunken fight. For some reason, such logic didn't occur to me during that whole busy night of searching. I suppose I wasn't thinking straight. I was still in shock from the women's gossip that Viktor had been dating Sveta in secret. For the entire time that we were poking around the bushes on the shores of the lake, my mind was concerned with rumours and gossip instead of saving Svetlana. There must have been a reason behind what people were saying. Dammit, even I felt they contained an element of truth. Why else would Sergei slam his brother in the face in the middle of his own wedding? There must be some substance to the gossip. Moreover, Sveta talked constantly about Viktor. She was his biggest fan. Be that as it may, how could a man go after his younger brother's girl! I couldn't get my head round it. I was running up and down the shore, overcome by such thoughts, when suddenly another memory came back to me. A while ago, Viktor had become jealous of the attention paid to Sveta by an officer from Naryn and had fought him. I had heard about it from someone I trusted, but at the time I had paid no attention. I figured Viktor was fighting to defend his brother's honour; But perhaps not?

* * *

Maybe it was the cold wind from the Boom Valley that helped, but after all that activity on the shore my anger subsided and the fire in my soul died out. It was all rumours, I told myself: Evil, empty, dirty rumours. Since there was no proof, I told myself to turn my back on such dirt. It would be strange if people didn't gossip about a beautiful girl like Sveta, so bright and sure of herself.

I think I pulled myself together, let go of my jealousy and starting hoping that Sveta was alright. But I also thought that I should get to the bottom of the gossip and find out the truth once and for all so that I could be at peace. If you can't find an inner calm and continue to doubt the one you love, then you'll forever be tormented by mental agony. Your eyes will become dull, the smile will leave your face and all that will be left of you is a shell. If you want to avoid that fate, you have to be absolutely sure of the one you love most of all.

Those reflections were the result of the strange and awful ending to Sveta's wedding. How could she and Sergei ever have a future together after such shame? It was impossible! That consolation came to me again and again, ever growing in strength. But another thought whined quietly in a far corner of my mind and its insistence became increasingly upsetting to me. The thought concerned Viktor.

Viktor didn't have his younger brother's height or build, but he was a prodigy on the guitar. He led a band and wrote songs and poems. He was a talented kid. Young and old, everyone in town knew his name. In particular, people respected him for his song "To My Father," which was tragic in both its melody and its words. Now would be a good time to tell the story of their legendary father, Peter Nikitich Samsonov, a man whose name lives on in people's hearts. There is no easy way of telling the story of Peter Nikitich, but I'll keep it short. An upsetting reminder of the cruelty of life; once you've heard it you'll never forget it. This is how it was told to me by Danil Grigorievich Cherkashin.

* * *

It happened a while ago. One day Peter Nikitich received a note from his younger brother Timofei, who was a game warden in the mountains.

"Petya, I've killed a lame boar. Why don't you come up? Bring everybody and we'll celebrate my 40th birthday. We're out of booze, so bring some with you. Timofei."

Timofei was Peter's only full brother, so he put his wife in their wagon which had only two wheels taken from a Moskvich car, and set off to visit him. His brother lived just twenty kilometres from Balykchy, but there were no roads to his home. He lived in a wooden house built by the government in a thickly forested ravine, with his wife and two young children, a son and a daughter.

That night the two brothers and their families made liver from the boar's fresh entrails and ate it together. It was a warm, happy celebration of the younger brother's fortieth birthday. Early the next morning they were awakened by a piercing scream. It was Timofei's wife. The whole family jumped out of bed and ran over to find the game warden lying dead in his bed, still a young man without a grey hair on his head. His cheeks were still rosy and he looked alive, but he was not breathing.

Peter Nikitich had come running in his underwear, still half asleep. He stamped his foot on the floor and bellowed "What misfortune is this?"

His wife tried to calm him down. "Quiet, you'll scare the children!"

Then the family began to weep silently, and it was a long time before they could regain their composure. Fate often works that way. We can never predict when our end will come, and often, when someone is settled and enjoying life, God decides it's time to take his soul.

At noon, Peter Nikitich announced "It's time to go!" The first shock had passed and the family was coming to terms with their loss.

Timofei's thin wife Katerina wiped her eyes anxiously. "Go where?"

"Back to town: to bury Tim."

"Timofei's not going anywhere. We'll lay him here."

"Have you lost your mind, Katerina? Bury my brother in the steppe? Our father is in the city cemetery. He will be at peace with our father."

Katerina was having none of it. She had always disliked her brother-in-law. In the past, there had been a serious feud, and afterwards, Timofei had taken up drinking and raising his hand on occasion to his wife or his brother.

Now Timofei lay silent. His heart had suddenly stopped and his body was growing cold. The latest argument between two people he loved, his wife and his brother, could no longer touch him. Peter Nikitich had no choice but to assert his authority, as head of the family. He shoved Katerina out of the way so hard that she fell, rolled Timofei's body in a rug, tied it with rope and with the help of his wife, Lyuda, carried the body to their cart.

"You can bury your own brother! I'm not coming!" Katerina held out for a while longer. Eventually Lyudmila convinced her to go with them, but Katerina, who was still under the influence of the samogon[1] from the night before, tore at her brother-in-law's nerves. She snarled at him and didn't want to get in the cart.

Furious and silent, Peter Nikitich hitched the horses and brought out the children, who were still wrapped in their blankets, sleeping sweetly. He laid them, next to their dead father, took up the reins and whipped the horses. The women sat behind him. Before setting off, they each knocked back a glass of samogon for the road. The day was overcast and foggy.

The track descended steeply and horses were having a hard time holding back the wobbling cart. Katerina was still grumbling.

"This was a stupid idea, Peter Nikitich. You should have listened to me! For goodness sake; you'll overturn this cart and kill me and my little ones!"

By then the children had woken up. When she heard her mother, Timofei's eight-year-old daughter started sobbing. Suddenly the scene was filled with the most unimaginable clamour.

---

1 Distilled liquor or moonshine

Peter Nikitich was knocked about as he tried desperately to hold back the horses' headlong descent. He was pale.

"All of you, shut up!" he roared over his shoulder.

Just then he noticed a grey, shadowy form flit past the yoke of the horse on the right. At first he thought it was a dog. A similar shape appeared on the left. The cart had arrived at the foot of the hill, where the track flattened out. The fog was thicker here but Peter Nikitich could see well enough to realize that they were under attack by a pack of wolves. The colour left his face and his heart stuck in his throat, but he did not show his fear.

Meanwhile, the horses had caught the predators' scent and took off. The cart leapt along the rocky road, threatening to toss out its passengers; two children, two women and a dead man! Peter Nikitich knew that the pack would kill them all in the blink of an eye.

"Go! Go!" he cried, lashing the horses with his whip. They were already running as fast as they could, but the cart was heavy and the track was muddy.

In early spring all predators' ribs stick out. They're starving. Enraged, the wolves were already biting the cart's rubber tyres. Soon they were nipping at the hot flesh of the exhausted horses.

Peter Nikitich struck the wolves with his whip several times, but they took no notice. It seemed to make them even more determined. By then both of the women sitting behind Peter Nikitich realized that they were completely surrounded by wolves and that the horses and everyone in the cart were just a hair's breadth from death. Both of them fell silent and froze in horror, their hearts stopping. Then, all of a sudden, Katerina let out a scream. Her mother's instinct had finally broken through her drunken haze.

"You've killed my children! You've killed my children, Peter Nikitich! God will punish you! You did it deliberately!"

Lyudmila, who was always level headed and rarely showed emotion, must also have lost all self -control in the face of their demise, for she began screaming with Katerina, "Drive the horses, Petya! Don't just sit there! Drive them faster!"

As he drove the horses as hard as they could go, with his heart racing, Peter Nikitich lost hope. His eyes rolled in his head, and he saw a wolf grab one of the horses by the hock and run alongside it without releasing its jaws. Two or three other wolves were jumping at the horses, trying to grasp at their throats.

At that moment Peter Nikitch lost it. No, he didn't lose it, but he pushed his whole life into the past, into the darkness, and made a leap towards the one weak ray of hope that could save them all. There was no alternative.

"Take the reins and drive them hard!"

For the rest of her life, Lyudmila would hear her husband's last words and recall his figure as he leapt like a bird of prey onto one of the wolves. Her ill-fated husband gave himself up for the wolves to devour.

The starving wolves gave up chasing the cart and fell on their victim, feasting on the hot blood. Human meat is a treat they do not often taste.

That is how Danil Cherkashin ended his story.

* * *

Viktor was very proud of the father who had sacrificed himself for his family, but no one ever heard Sergei, the younger boy, mention it. Anyone who knew them would comment: Two brothers, two different personalities. Such was the will of

Mother Nature, who gives birth to all living things.

It took Viktor years to write "To My Father," and all his work paid off. Both the words and the melody were haunting. When he first sang it in public, there wasn't a dry eye in the room. You couldn't listen to the song without crying. I had heard it many times. The words, the music, the way he sang it all came together in deep harmony. Viktor's song expressed the spiritual life of a young man, his sorrow and pain, his love for his father, and his pride. The son revealed all that was good in Peter Nikitch and sang of his greatness. One of the reviews which I read described Viktor's song was an eternal monument to his father. The city papers picked up that review and printed it again and again.

And now Viktor the singer was sitting in jail with his brother. I wondered how he felt. What was going through his mind? What were his sorrows? Did he feel that he had deserved being hit in the face by his brother, in public? Or did he regret getting involved in that ridiculous fight? Was he pity his brother, who had lost his mind to drugs? Was he worried about what would become of Svetlana? Had their feelings for each other grown deeper, perhaps? Could it be that Viktor was glad that Sveta's wedding had been ruined because he hoped that now the beautiful girl would be his? Probably not: As long as Sergei was alive, I was sure that Viktor had no chance. That was my view. I hoped they wouldn't end up killing each other. It could happen. The Russian temperament is capable of anything. Nothing can curb it.

* * *

Against all hope, three days of searching turned up nothing. Svetlana Cherkashina was nowhere to be found. She had completely disappeared. We presumed that if she were alive she'd give some kind of sign of, maybe a phone call or note. But there was no news. After a while, the police search began to lose steam. Sveta's father and mother despaired. The city papers kept rehashing the sensational news of the missing bride. What else could they do? She was gone.

I can't comment about anyone else, but my feelings for her became openly transparent and I became very self-conscious. I felt the sympathetic looks when I walked into my office. Nobody said what they were thinking, but their eyes were full of pity. Even without anything being said, it was obvious. Everyone knew I was the third wheel. I suppose they were laughing inside. Maybe they were laughing at me for running around searching for Svetlana, who had dropped me for another man. I knew I was being stupid, but I stayed with the search party. My one goal, after all the strange and scandalous things that had happened, was to see the person I loved one more time, to look her in the eye. I hoped that would reveal to me what kind of person she really was. Perhaps Svetlana would still be my mysterious, pure beloved...or perhaps I would become disillusioned and come to hate her. But I couldn't be at peace until I found out. I had to find an answer to the question once and for all.

Meanwhile, we heard that Sergei and his friends had been charged with hooliganism and that an investigation was underway. At least a dozen of the people from the restaurant ended up in hospital. The investigator called in people from our company who knew Sveta to answer questions. When they came back, they reported that everyone was giving evidence against Sergei. They also said that the investigator wanted to prove that Sveta had also been involved in the fight. I too, expected to be called in to answer questions, but for the time being no one contacted me.

Even the most painful experiences lose their sharp edge over time and are eventually absorbed by everyday life. A hazy web slowly winds itself around all recollection of the event and its colours fade as it eventually disappears from memory into the past.

And in this case, even though everyone had been worried and upset, over time, most of the people in town began to forget about Sveta's disappearance. All of them had their own worries and cares.

The investigation dragged on for more than a month. Finally, one day Viktor called to ask to see me at work. It felt like I had been waiting for his call, probably because I knew that he had been released, while Sergei was still in jail. If he really cared about Sveta, he would try to do something and that meant he would have to come to me. He did. But I hadn't known how his call would affect me. I began to feel angry with myself. How could I begin to talk calmly with a bastard who seduced his own brother's girlfriend while his brother was in the army? What kind of man did that? He wasn't a man at all!

Just then the door opened. It was Viktor. He had come to see me in the past about his concerts, and for Sveta's sake I had always helped him out.

"Come in," I said coldly.

The stern look on my face made him shy, and he held out his hand uncomfortably without saying anything.

I gave his hand a halfhearted shake and asked him bluntly "Why are you two brothers acting like a pair of fools?"

Viktor stared at me for a long time. I didn't see any anger or pity in his eyes, but there was something hidden in his face. He didn't seem to know how to express what he was thinking.

"Let's hear it." I pressed, "Why are you here?" I wanted

to make it clear that of the two of us, I was the one with nothing on my conscience.

Viktor sat with his head bowed. After a while he looked away from me. Then, because he knew there was no getting away from it and there was no one else he could tell, he told me an unbelievable story.

It sounded unconvincing but by then, because I had already seen much stranger things, I had to take Viktor at his word. Is there anything more complicated that human fate? People's experiences, the world over, are different from each other; unmatched, unique! But when you take a close look at any of them, you see more sorrow than joy; agonies piled one on top of another. After all, anguish has been the essence of human existence on Earth from the very beginning.

Truly, those were the thoughts that came to me after I heard what Viktor had to say. At first I listened to him with obvious suspicion. Why should I believe him? We businessmen are well familiar with sob stories being used as tedious excuses. People will tell you all kinds of horrors and, at the end of the story, ask you for help. It's always money they need. Viktor had apparently hit on the idea of using the search for Sveta as a way of getting money out of me. He assumed that I couldn't refuse. Maybe I would give him something, but I'd give him a piece of my mind first.

When he began, my body tensed and I tapped my pencil on my desk as I listened. I don't remember when I threw down my pencil, but after a while I was engrossed with his story, my mouth agape. Suddenly I took charge.

"Are you a man or not? Don't whine. Get on with the story!" I wanted to encourage Viktor. He was uncomfortable. He kept wiping his eyes. His voice wavered and his sighing and sniffling kept interrupting his tale.

In a nutshell, this is what he told me.

The Cherkashins and Samsonovs had been exiled to Kyrgyzstan for their anti-slavery views 140 years ago, during the reign of Alexander II. The families were closely related. Since then, they had known times good and bad, peppered with joy and feuds. Not long ago, when both Danil Grigorievich Cherkashin and Peter Nikitich Samsonov were still alive, the relationship between the two families took a serious turn for the worse. And what had sparked this? Well, it was the usual curse of vodka. Everyone was drunk on some holiday or other and Danil Cherkashin stabbed Katerina's brother Konstantin in the stomach. According to testimony given in court, Konstantin had been swearing at his brother-in-law and dragging him by the collar, and had even kicked him in the stomach with his boot. However, the court did not take these circumstances into account because Konstantin died in hospital. Peter Nikitich Samsonov gave evidence against Konstantin in court, and from that moment onwards, his sister-in-law Katerina became his sworn enemy. His younger brother Timofei took his wife's side. They worked together to make sure that Danil was sentenced to ten years.

Prison is prison. The jailors don't care whether you landed there by accident or whether you were an angel or a devil before prison. Everyone is termed a criminal. But even behind the barbed wire Danil Cherkashin's carpentry skills stood him in good stead. He worked tirelessly, never laying down his saw and axe, hoping to walk out of prison alive and healthy in five years instead of ten. In time, all the early release paperwork was ready. The only problem was that he would have to give money to the prison warden. Five thousand! And who was expected to come up with that sum of money: His family in Balykchy, including the Samsonovs! It took a long time to amass. Cherkashin was already exhausted by the wait, but he kept on working continuously. Then the old saying about trouble never being far away proved itself again. The poor man was raped by a couple of younger convicts. He tried to escape from them, but they beat him until he lost consciousness. Danil Grigorievich ended up in hospital.

The incident had the potential to cause serious trouble for the warden because the rapists had left their prison sector unhindered in order to commit the crime. It was an obvious violation of prison regulations and the administration was at fault.

The prison bosses leapt into action. They got Cherkashin back on his feet and, after warning him not to file an official complaint, immediately processed his early release for good behavior and hard work.

* * *

Danil Cherkashin returned home half dead. The injuries to his arms and legs had healed, but the effects of the concussion caused him much suffering. During the day he somehow managed to get along, but terrible headaches kept him up all night.

It wasn't just the headaches that tortured him at night. His spirit could not bear the shame he had suffered at his age.

There had been an axe in his hand. Why hadn't he whacked off the head of one of those bastards? He wept into his pillow in anguish.

The past is the past. That's what he told himself. But he discovered that his humiliation and shame did not weaken with time. They were growing. If only word of his shame had not reached Balykchy, but it had. It most certainly had. Another man from town, who was doing ten years for killing his wife, called home with the news. In all his years of quietly earning a living by his trade, Danil could never have imagined that fate would bring him such misfortune! He had a little man's big hope that one day the headaches would stop and he could go back to his old life...

Revenge knows no human limits. Katerina thought that her brother Konstantin was not sufficiently atoned for, so she began to raise a stink.

"Why did they let him out early? I'm going to complain. I'll write to the Central Committee."

Her husband Timofei was completely on her side. The feud between the Samsonovs and the Cherkashins flared up again.

Unable to bear it, Danil tried to kill himself on several occasions, but some people are tougher than dogs and can't seem to die. He tried swallowing poison and hanging himself, but it never worked. Each time his wife managed to save him. Eventually it got so bad that Zoya Ivanovna wouldn't take her eyes off him.

"You fool! Haven't you had enough death yet? Take pity on your daughter!" she wept, her arms around five-year-old Svetlana. "Do you think God will forgive you for making an orphan of her? Use your head!"

Danil had thought about all of this, but what was the alternative? His two families were again enemies and the old hatred had returned. Only his death could put an end to it. So what if Zoya was constantly shoving his paternal responsibilities to his only daughter in his face? She'd grow up just fine, there was no question of that, and she'd find her own happiness. She'd have a mother and a bunch of relatives who wouldn't let anything happen to her.

One day when Danil was hiding from his wife and giving in to a bout of tears, his Kyrgyz friend Asankul came by to visit. They had been childhood friends who had gone to school and played football together. It was Asankul who had taken Danil to prison, with tears in his eyes.

After listening to Cherkashin's sorrow from beginning to end, Asankul suddenly made an unexpected suggestion.

"When we Kyrgyz find ourselves in a tough spot like the one you're in, here's what we do. We become in-laws. Do you know how Kyrgyz do that?"

"I've heard."

"Then listen. You have a daughter, Sveta. Peter Samsonov has two sons, Viktor and Sergei. I'll talk Peter into it. Let him ask for your daughter's hand for one of his sons and put earrings in her ears. I think that the older one, Viktor, is the best choice. Once you're in-laws you can't feud. You'll have to respect each other. The children will embody the family ties between you. There's no alternative. See?"

Danil had listened to Asankul with his right hand over his heart and his head lowered. Now he looked up at his friend doubtfully and shrugged his shoulders.

After a while he croaked, "Viktor isn't Timofei's son. He's Peter's."

"So what: Timofei and Peter are brothers. Let Timofei be your in-law and that disagreeable wife of his will be your in-law, too. What can they do about it? Not a thing!"

"You seem to assume that Russians are just like Kyrgyz, Asankul."

"Come on, Danik, all of you turned into Kyrgyz long ago. Look at all the ties between us. Peter's even more of a Kyrgyz than you are. I know him. He'll be more than pleased when I tell him my idea. Then he can help me bring his brother round.

Once Timofei's on board his woman can't get out of it. If she opens her mouth, Tima will knock back a drink and beat the leather out of her."

"I don't need that. God forbid. She's already black hearted. She'd as soon put Timofei in prison as say 'good morning' to him."

"Don't worry, Danik. There are plenty of people around. We're here. If that bastard Konstantin hadn't died, may the devil take him, we never would have let them pack you off to prison. It was his fault, wasn't it? He kicked you first."

Danil said nothing and kept his head down. He didn't want to think about his in-law Konstantin. What was the point? He preferred to give some thought to Asankul's proposal.

Finally he raised his head. "You talk to Petro."

* * *

Here's how things progressed. Asankul was able to convince Peter, who talked Timofei into the plan. Katerina would hear none of it. So the men got together, boiled up a strong soup made from local marinkas fish, drank too much vodka and hung silver earrings in five-year-old Sveta's ears. They then headed off. The child loved the trinkets so much that she wore them without taking them off until she had grown up.

Whenever anyone asked her who she would marry, she would lisp "Vikor" and everyone would fall down laughing. Viktor was already a teenager, and he raised hell at home when he heard the story.

"The whole school is already calling me and Sveta 'bride and groom.' I can't believe you did that, Papa!"

"Don't pay any attention to them. Let them talk," Peter told his son.

"Sure. Let them talk. They're laughing at us. I won't go back to school. I'm not going to study."

Peter couldn't think of how to best to respond. His wife Lyudmila gloated.

"What nonsense! You don't want to go to school just because some folk are wagging their tongues?"

Peter was privately more upset with his wife than his son. He knew she and Katerina were the ones who had spread the rumours to the school.

"I won't go anymore."

"You've gone and ruined your son because you let some backward Kyrgyz talk you into something stupid."

It wasn't the first time his wife had said things of this sort. His rational, reserved Lyudmila suddenly started sounding like his argumentative sister-in-law Katerina. Her empty criticism made Peter furious, sometimes to the point where he blew up. He slammed the door and left. That was not a good sign. Aware of what it meant, that night Lyudmila slept lightly with a son on either side of her. Peter came home when the sun was already high. She reckoned that he'd got drunk first thing in the morning in order to give her what-for while the boys were in school. But when Peter got there, Viktor was still at home. He hadn't gone to school.

He grabbed his son by the shirt, pulled him out of bed and tossed him on the floor. "You rascal: Don't want to go to school? Fine! Then come with me. You're going to haul shit."

In the heat of his anger, Peter revealed something that he had always kept hidden from his children: He worked as a sewer cleaner for the city. He had never told anyone this, especially his children. But now he let loose his anger and took his older son to work with him for two days in a row, making him haul the sickly, foul, ribbed hoses used for pumping the products of human waste. There was nothing that could wash away the smell.

On the third day, Peter raised his son's face by his chin. "Will you go back to school?" Viktor closed his eyes and said nothing.

"Go." He shoved him forward. "And I don't want to hear another word about it. If you don't finish school, you'll spend your whole life dragging stinking hoses. Hear me?"

Without a word, Viktor headed home. He hadn't said if he was going back to school or not.

* * *

"How did Svetlana react to the teasing?" I asked when Viktor's story started to dry up.

I felt that without that knowledge I'd never understand the feud between the brothers. I had to figure it out. Viktor had a gentle nature; he wrote songs, sang and played music, but he wasn't much of a talker. And he kept some things to himself. When we first started talking he had avoided my direct question about why Sergei had whacked a plate across his face, and he was still avoiding an answer. Moreover, his speech began to ramble and sound incoherent. But if you assembled all of the disconnected, jumbled things he told me, it would read like this:

At school, Sveta was number one in terms of height, looks and grades. She always held her head high and carried herself with grace and dignity. She was a fun-loving girl, and when she first heard the "bride and groom" jokes she burst out laughing and then cracked the kid who had teased her over the head with a book. She hit him so hard that he gave up on the spot. That was the method she employed from then on. Whenever anyone bothered her, she would simply and without a word, hit them in the face with a book or notebook, and keep on walking.

No one, neither the boys nor the girls, could figure out what it meant. Was she admitting to the engagement or denying it? And she never got embarrassed. No, she just went on being her bold, energetic self.

But Viktor was a boy, and the teasing upset him. He wanted the Earth to open and swallow him up. For days on end he avoided his relatives and spent all his time studying. Whenever he ran into Sveta, he would blush to the roots of his hair and run off. He never went to dances because he was afraid of seeing his "bride." He turned over his band to another guy and hid out at home, never poking his nose outside. In the past, he had always hung around Sveta, dragging her to rock concerts in the evening making her sing backup, walking her home every day and whenever he saw the opportunity, wrap his arm tightly around her. That was the personality God gave him. But now he was hiding at home from his betrothed.

Meanwhile, Svetlana started holding hands with his younger brother Sergei. At first she treated him like just another relative. They went out together in the evenings and walked home together, since they were almost neighbours. Compared to Viktor, Sergei was good-looking and tall enough for Svetlana. He was quiet and reserved; traits that drove the girls wild. There wasn't a girl in the school who didn't throw looks his direction, but Svetlana left them all broken hearted when she effortlessly nabbed him.

There's no understanding the human heart: it's like a dark forest. Viktor had run away from Sveta when he heard about their childhood betrothal, but as soon as she chose his brother to be her boyfriend, he began trailing her like a shadow. He started inviting her to concerts again, finding all sorts of reasons to give her flowers and taking her to the shore of the lake to listen to music. Whenever Sergei was away, Viktor appeared at her side. Word of mouth carried news of this unusual situation all around town until it finally reached the boys' parents.

Peter Nikitich called Sergei to him. "My son, can't you find another girl?"

"Why?"

"People are saying that you're going out with the daughter of our relatives, the Cherkashins."

"So what: Maybe I am."

"Then don't! It'll cause a lot of trouble. We'll start killing each other again. It took a lot of effort to calm everyone down, and I don't want my son reawakening the feud. You're not kids anymore. Think about what you're doing!"

"Tell that to Viktor, Papa."

"I won't tell Viktor any such thing. He's in a different situation, one which arose when you all were little."

"What happened?"

"You've never heard?"

"No."

"They're betrothed. We put earrings in Sveta's ears."

"Who's betrothed?"

"Viktor and Sveta."

Sergei laughed. "Just like the backward aborigines?"

"What else could we do? And it's a good thing it worked."

"I bet Sveta threw those earrings out years ago. So forget it, Papa!"

"I don't believe that. Sveta's not that kind of girl."

"Papa, I'll buy you a hundred of those earrings so you can put them on anyone you want. Hang them from your nose, for all I care. But leave Sveta alone. We know what we're doing. Is that clear?"

Peter Nikitich began to shake. His face went white and his throat tightened. For a while he sat in silence. Then he spoke:

"Son, I am your father. May God keep us from a catastrophe! I will destroy one of you. Remember that!"

* * *

So once upon a time, poor Peter Nikitich was angry at his sons, but where is he now? Where are his remains, his ashes? He was not even buried, and not a trace of him is left on this Earth.

The next morning, when people heard about the terrible tragedy, they went out to look for Peter's remains. They returned home empty-handed. There was nothing to be found. His two sons spent a week combing the field where their father had died, but they too, came home with nothing. Lethally hungry by spring, the wolves must have devoured his entire body, his bones included. The Creator had willed that one of our characters, Peter Nikitich Samsonov, would never find peace on Earth. There would be no plot of ground for him and no gravestone. But his virtue lived on in people's memories. For what it's worth, telling it well or telling it poorly, I have tried to express on paper, what kind of man he was.

I can't bring myself to hope that he found a soft resting place on Earth. There will be no eternal peace for Peter Nikitich, no mound of soil to cover him. His dust is nowhere to be found. In hopeless situations like these, the Kyrgyz say "may his soul abide in paradise." That's it. We simply hope that when a man's heart stops beating, his soul, weightless and invisible, finds its way to paradise and stays there eternally. And since the soul is eternal and immortal, sooner or later it will return to this earthly life in a new body.

* * *

Viktor's story was taking too long.

I was annoyed. I couldn't stop myself from interrupting. "Do you know where Svetlana is? Spit it out."

"I'd have a guess."

"Where?"

Viktor looked at me suspiciously. He probably wondered why I was so emotionally involved. I was boiling inside. We had a missing person to find and just talking about her wouldn't help!

"Well? Where do you think she is?" I repeated, my eyes drilling holes in Viktor.

"You want the truth?"

"No, just lie to me! Sveta is my employee!"

"I heard that you asked her parents for her hand."

I choked. "That doesn't matter. What matters is finding her. Don't you get it?"

"Yeah, I get it."

"Then talk faster. Tell me what you know, if you do know anything."

"I think someone took her to Naryn."

"Who?"

"One particular Chechen guy."

"Who did you say?"

"Can you go to Naryn with me?"

"The same Chechen you got into a fight with?"

"Right."

"Was Sveta dating him, too?"

"Sveta was going out with all of us. She wouldn't pass anybody over."

I jumped up, my heart pounding. "What a slut!"

"Who? Sveta?" Viktor looked surprised.

"Who else?"

"She has the right to choose her man. We men always think we do the choosing, but we're actually the ones who get chosen."

I stood staring at him in shock. "Is that your philosophy? Is that what you came here to tell me?"

"I came to ask you if you'll go to Naryn with me."

"How many other men did Sveta have? Tell me!"

"It's hard to say. When Sergei went into the army he entrusted her to me and told me to keep watch over her. Why should I watch over her? She was betrothed to me. Sveta never denied it. She told me 'I'm yours.' We slept together."

"You slept together and then she threw away the earrings?" I didn't know what to say.

"Sergei made that up. She's got the earrings hidden in her trunk."

"I don't get any of this, with God as my witness. You're brothers. You can't share the same girl. Did Sveta sleep with Sergei, too?"

"Yes. But she never let anyone touch her."

"How do you know that?" I exploded.

"I just know. She didn't let me touch her either."

I was furious, but I laughed. "She didn't give you anything, but how do you know what she did with others? Idiot!"

"I don't know. Maybe she gave you a gift?"

I shut my mouth. I was in the same boat as Viktor. I was furious to discover that my most sacred feelings for Sveta were apparently public knowledge. I was shocked and ashamed at the same time. To my mind, you should never speak about such intimate feelings. They should weave a nest in the hearts of the two people concerned and live there like birds! Otherwise the death of great love is inevitable!

Viktor interrupted my thoughts. "Will you go to Naryn?"

"Why Naryn?"

"To look for Sveta. The Chechen serves in a border division."

I couldn't get my thoughts in order for a long time.

"How could Sveta end up in Naryn?" I finally asked him.

"Some people saw the Chechen waiting in his car around the corner from the restaurant; On the night of the wedding."

"For the love of God! You can shoot me if I've understood a thing you've said. Who invited the Chechen? Sveta? How could she invite him to her wedding with Sergei? How could anyone be so foolish?"

"I guess it happens."

"Who told you this nonsense?"

"Wait! I doubt that Sveta did invite the Chechen. He was hoping for a miracle, waiting for something. That's what I think."

I can't stand people whose thoughts are disorganized and who can't tell a straight story, even if I do feel sorry for them sometimes. I was enraged that I'd already spent two hours talking to Viktor and still didn't have any clear answers to my questions.

"Where did you fight the guy? Can you at least tell me that?"

"What's the big deal? He came down to Balykchy from Naryn every week to buy groceries for his border post. He ran into Sveta. I don't know how or where. He once even drove her out to Naryn."

"Who? Sveta?"

"Yeah."

My blood boiled and rushed to my face. Viktor noticed. He smiled mysteriously.

"And?" I mumbled, barely able to contain myself.

"Then he came to a dance one night. I was playing with my band. He paid us and kept requesting the same song, the Lezginka. He and Sveta danced together oblivious to anyone else. Nobody could touch them. At first I was surprised at how wildly Sveta danced. The Chechen was good, too. Then we all got angry with the Chechen. We were mad that he acted like none of us even existed.

"Oleg from our band said, 'Let's get him!' He too was head over heels in love with Sveta. Before the dancing was even over, we dragged the Chechen behind the café and attacked him, but he tossed the four of us off like it was nothing. Bastard! We ripped his shirt. Then we saw the tattoo over his heart: a portrait of Sveta."

"What colour was it?" I asked stupidly.

"Orange. They say that's the colour of God."

"Did he stop coming on to Sveta after that?"

"I don't know. The cops arrested us. Sveta had called them. We got five months because he was an army officer."

"So he kept coming to see Sveta?"

"Maybe. Some people say he's a sorcerer. They say he knows black magic."

"Do you think Sveta slept with him, too?"

"She could have. She loved him."

"She loved him?"

"I noticed it once. Back when Sveta was still in technical school. They both disappeared for two days. Sveta's father yelled at me. He thought I was doing a bad job watching over my betrothed. But what could I do? Sveta's not an animal I can keep on a leash, you know?"

"But don't you love her?"

"Sure."

"So you should have kept an eye on her!"

"She liked Sergei better."

"What about the Chechen?"

"She liked him better, too. He's not a regular guy. There's something about him. And I don't think it's something good."

I was thoroughly upset that I had spent so much time listening to the empty talk of this wandering idiot. I don't know with whom I was angrier, Viktor or Sveta, who apparently could fall for anyone who smiled at her. I decided to put an end to this conversation, which was of no value to me. I stood up and prepared to leave.

If Sveta really had run off with the Chechen, then it was time for me to forget about all the times I had wasted on the foolish woman and feelings in which I had stupidly indulged; feelings which made me a laughing stock in town. I would never think about it or talk about it again!

"Thanks for the story. The way you tell it, Sveta loved all of us but in the end she chose this Chechen." My red-rimmed eyes drilled Viktor. "I hope she's happy with him. You can tell her that!"

"That isn't right. She shouldn't stay with the Chechen. He has the devil inside him. We have to find her. Let her tell us the whole story. We have to go to the border post."

"I wouldn't go there for anything in the world!" I yelled.

"Then send me. Sveta will be yours. I know it."

"What?"

"I'm sure of it. She wants a rich, stable husband. She still doesn't know who that Chechen is."

"I'm not that rich. But maybe I can send you to Naryn."

In an instant, I softened. Seeing that, Viktor jumped up and gave me his hand. As soon as he had the money, he ran out the door and I fell back into my chair. My head ached. I didn't understand anything. I didn't know anything. I couldn't even begin to guess. God only knew why that half-wit Viktor really wanted to go to Naryn.

I massaged my head and decided that it didn't matter. Sergei was the real danger. What evil things was he cooking up in jail? As the instigator of a legendary fight, he had it coming when he got out. Either he would kill someone, or someone would kill him. He couldn't escape it. His cool, detached nature was capable of terrible things. Who would end up his hostage: his brother Viktor, Sveta, or maybe the Chechen? It was hard to say. Sergei was quiet when he was sober, but who knew what he was like under the influence of drugs? Who would he blame? Who would he choose as his victim?

You never know in which direction a brain poisoned with cocaine will head.

Once Viktor had left for Naryn, I was seized by a single hope. If Sveta was still alive, then she would call someone, either me or her parents. As my employee, she had to let me know where she was! I was always waiting for this call, and my mobile phone never left my pocket. I was also trying to avoid dwelling on one particular thought: Sveta's feelings for me. Hope is stubborn. Once it takes hold, you can't get rid of it easily! It lives on in your soul, torturing you as it pulls on your heartstrings.

After everything that had happened, it was time for me, old fool that I was, to acknowledge that Sveta didn't love me. She had never loved me. She was just playing with me. Whenever the thought appeared, I ran from it like a scared rabbit. I tried to distract myself with work, taking on extra responsibilities. I even made frequent appearances at the casino and went to nightclubs with friends, although I had never set foot in such places before. It was useless. The splinter was stuck deep in my heart. After a while, I began to get used to it. Since there was no news from Sveta, that meant she hadn't even thought of me or even her job. That's what I told myself, but another thought would not let me go. It held my hope like a fish on a line. What if she's lying injured and helpless in a hospital somewhere? Wait. Don't lose your mind. Go and look for her! But I had no idea where to look. All I could do was await news from Viktor. But would that news give me peace if I found out that Sveta really had run off to Naryn with someone?

There I sat, melancholy and weak, in such a foul mood that I didn't want to work or eat lunch. Suddenly the door opened and in walked none other than Sveta's father, Danil Grigorievich. He was drunk and looked like he'd been crying. He tripped over the threshold and fell towards me with his hand extended.

"Sveta's been found," he said.

I jumped up in surprise. "Where?"

"I need money. Money!"

"What money?" I didn't know what he was talking about.

"Regular green money. Yankee money!"

"Who wants it?"

"The damn gangsters! Who else? Son, do you understand what I'm saying? They shoot people like dogs. That's what they told me. They said they'd shoot my daughter like a dog!"

"I don't' understand, Danil Grigorievich."

Danil Grigorievich rubbed his eyes with his fists.

"You loved my Sveta, didn't you?"

I said nothing, eyes downcast.

"I know you did, you devil. Sveta loved you too, the poor fool. That's why you have to give me the money. Otherwise they'll kill your Sveta. If my daughter survives, she'll pay you back. Don't be a coward."

"Explain who you're talking about."

"Gangsters!" the old man yelled, pounding his fist on my desk.

"Some gangsters kidnapped Sveta?"

"What's wrong with you? How many times do I have to explain?"

"How much do they want?"

"I'm an old man. I don't have that kind of money."

"I asked you how much they want."

"One million," he said, turning his red eyes to my face.

"One million what? Soms? Dollars?"

"How do I know? You talk to the bastards, damn it!"

It was obvious that Danil Grigorievich had just knocked back a full glass of vodka. He started to break down and use foul language. But still I listened to him, trying to piece together what had happened."

By morning he had sobered up and I got more details when I talked to him again. Then I went to see the chief of the city police. We decided to agree to the conditions the gangsters had given when they called Sveta's father. We didn't have to wait long. That day they called again and told him when and where to bring the money. We were to put a million soms in a plastic bag and hang it on the end of the city pier, which projects far over the lake. They would leave Sveta there in a rowing boat as soon as they had counted the money.

Fate brought me and my old acquaintance, the mustached Major, together again. He was in charge of the group dealing with our case. Sveta's father wasn't happy about it. He whispered to me that the Major was an idiot, incapable of doing anything right. Apparently he had never liked the officer, who was a bit of a loose cannon.

"Before we give them any money I have to hear my daughter's voice," Danil Grigorievich loudly asserted, facing me instead of the Major.

"Don't interfere in the operation, old man. We have to catch these gangsters whether or not you hear your daughter," retorted the Major. He then turned his back on us.

"See? They aren't even trying to get my daughter back! They're looking for something else!"

I was stuck in the middle. "Danil Grigorievich, let the police do their job. We mustn't interfere!

* * *

It was already four in the morning. The tourist season was over. We sat in a police van behind the fence of the Tolkun resort. Through a crack in the fence we had a perfect view of the pier. Sveta's stubborn father had insisted that we take him with us. It was almost five o'clock when the phone in his pocked beeped. The old man didn't hear it. I elbowed him.

"Hello!" he barked. Then he listened, holding his breath. Suddenly he leapt out of the van and started jumping around like a madman.

"Don't do it! Don't kill her! She's all I have! Oh God! Oh God! What did she ever do to you? Drown me instead! Take me!"

We knew it was the gangsters calling. What could we do?

"Was it them?" I asked, grabbing the old man by the shoulder as soon as he put away his phone. Danil Grigorievich stood frozen like a statue.

"The bastards saw everything," he finally mumbled.

After a pause, he added, "They saw us sitting here. And they saw the police speed boat lying in wait, and the boat under the pier. They saw everything. I told you that asshole Major never gets anything right. And he's probably asleep down in the boat. I'll railroad the bastard. If they drown my daughter, I'll railroad him!"

"Did they say they'd drown her?"

"Of course they did. And they will! They didn't get the money. They'll just toss her in the water and sail off! We'll never catch them! They called me an old ass. They said they'll cut off my head and stick it up my ass because I went to the police. God damn it."

"Don't lose it, Danil Grigorievich. Let's find a way out of this. We have to do it before dawn."

"You make me laugh, son. What way out? They told me to put the money in a waterproof bag and put it in a box in a field outside town."

"Is there water in the box?"

"How do I know?"

"When are you supposed to do this?"

"Right now and quickly. They told me to go alone. If anything isn't right, they'll shoot me there and then."

"What about Svetlana? How will they give her back?"

"I don't know," Danil Grigorievich looked at me sorrowfully.

"You should have asked. That's the most important thing. How are they going to return your daughter?"

"I was confused." He bowed his head.

The Major walked up to us. When he heard the new terms, he started talking rapidly about surrounding the box. At that point, Danil Grigorievich exploded.

"You can't surround criminals. They always surround you. You want me to lose my daughter! Do you understand what I'm saying? Have some fear of God. I'm going alone. Give me that bag. I'll do it myself!"

We watched what went on from a window in a building

on the edge of town. It was all we could do. As it turned out, the gangsters had worked out a detailed plan well in advance. We realized that later. The police had cars ready and waiting so they could catch up with the gangsters after the handover, but in an instant, the whole operation fell shamefully apart. No sooner had Danil Grigorievich hobbled up to the tall box, than a man in a mask jumped out from behind it, grabbed the blue bag from the old man and disappeared behind the box again. He had a motorcycle waiting for him nearby.

"Go!" Stunned, the Major called for his men to hurry. Unfortunately, there was nowhere for them to go. Their cars would have to make a detour of at least twenty kilometers to reach the nearest bridge.

* * *

Several days passed. There was no news from Viktor, who had gone to Naryn. The police, who had managed to lose a large sum of my money to the gangsters, were also keeping quiet. In the summer you can't move without running into a cop, but perhaps not surprisingly when winter comes, they're nowhere to be found.

I heard that Sergei Samsonov's case had already been sent to court. There were rumours that one of the people involved in the fight had died and the prosecutor wanted to pin the murder on Sergei. Otherwise the police would have an unsolved murder on their hands.

With each passing day, my depression grew. This I knew, without the need to consult any doctor or psychologist. At work I felt ashamed. I couldn't look people in the eye. Sveta had left all of us, especially me, in a terrible state. We still had no idea if she were alive or dead, but now the whole neighbourhood knew that she had thrown over all of her suitors. I can't speak for anyone else, but I had a hard time coping with people's barely hidden laughter. Sometimes terrible thoughts came to me during my sleepless nights: if Sveta was never found alive, then our universal shame would eventually recede into memory. Is it ever possible to know someone completely? I don't believe there is. Deep down, all of us hoped for the best, myself included. Maybe the missing girl was lying in a hospital somewhere and would come back to work once she had recovered. Maybe our relationship would straighten itself out somehow. Hope burned low, but it was there. Even though this isn't the kind of thing you talk about openly, it feels as though everyone who looks at you can see your shame. I say this because I've been through it. How else could I know such humiliation?

* * *

At last I heard a rumour that Viktor, who had gone to Naryn before the onset of winter, had only returned to Balykchy in the spring. He was admitted to hospital immediately. No one knew where he had come from. People said he had stopped talking, wouldn't speak to anyone, and was all skin and bones.

My employees wanted to visit him and ask him about Sveta but the doctor wouldn't let them in. I had no desire to go to him. I suppose that since our memorable last meeting, the drama which had been torturing me had reached a final conclusion. But as it turned out, there were mind-bending secrets waiting to cause me deep concern. I was shocked by a new twist in the story. The Russians have a witty proverb: "live a century and learn a century, but you'll still die a fool." That tract of folk wisdom points to the very root of human nature. You can master any science or any art and still not find the answer to the human mystery. I don't believe it's possible. I suppose that one of a professional writer's objectives is to solve this mystery, but you can see for yourselves where that leads. None of history's greatest philosophers have even been able to draw back the curtain on this mystery.

Be that as it may, I still feel bound to tell my readers how this awful drama ended. I will write it as it was explained to me by Viktor, changing it only to bring a measure of logic and order to his often confused narrative, which resulted from the fact that his mind was not the same after he had suffered concussion.

* * *

"Are you here to see me?" Viktor asked. He stared at me blankly from his hospital bed.

I squirmed inside. Previously, it had always been his custom to address me in the polite form, but now he hit me squarely with familiarity. He didn't seem to notice the difference. He'd had a serious concussion. His eyes were dull and lifeless, as if the fire in them had been extinguished.

"You asked to see me. Don't you recognize me? I'm the Company President. Samat Sadykov!"

Something flickered in Viktor's eyes. "I remember. You gave me money. I know you need Sveta. She's living it up with some Chechens in the next world. She listens to music every day. Music is the only thing that can heal her pain. It can't help me. I can't play music anymore. I lost my ear."

He began to cry. It took him a while to regain his composure.

"Do you know Brahms' Hungarian Dances? When Sveta listens to Brahms, the Chechen lights a candle and dances for her. When I look in the mirror I can see them there; in the next world."

I was afraid. "In the next world: Do you mean they're no longer here in this world? Are they dead?"

Back in the winter I had heard a rumour that they had drowned in the river on their way to Naryn.

"They are in the next world just as they are in this world," Viktor said. He pressed his hands to his head. He was angry with me.

"Are they in Naryn?"

Viktor choked with laughter. Then he gave me a searching stare. "They're in Ichkeria!" He was annoyed. "How can you be so stupid? Don't you understand?"

I nodded quickly. There was no other way to calm him down. It appeared to satisfy him. His annoyance subsided.

"I lived with them in Ichkeria. There were a lot of people at their wedding. Just like the Kyrgyz do, they tied a kerchief on her head and put her in a long dress. They grilled up a feast!"

I interrupted him. "Did Sveta go to Ichkeria voluntarily?"

"Sveta's glowing! She's happy!"

When he said that, I didn't need a mirror to know that my face had gone pale. A burning cold gripped my body. In an instant I came to hate Sveta's name. My emotions revolted. I think Viktor noticed.

"Sveta loves you," he said. It sounded mocking.

My nerves were on edge. I looked over my shoulder. Perhaps I should leave, but something held me back. I decided to listen to the end of his story no matter what. If poor Sveta had made a terrible mistake in marrying some Chechen, then she deserved all she got. And part of my need for revenge would be satisfied. Otherwise I felt that her insult would remain in my soul and ruin my whole life.

Viktor kept drifting off and waking up again. They must

have given him a hefty dose of something to help him sleep. He couldn't raise his head. I plumped up his pillow.

He began to mumble. "The mountains in Chechnya are low, not like our mountains. I saw it in the mirror: Stray dogs, Wandering cows, Chechens. They aren't afraid of death. Vainakhs! Viktor's eyes widened. "When Vainakhs hear of war they dance and are joyful. Vainakhs! Machine guns! Rifles! Hand grenades! Bombs!

Viktor was upset again. His eyes were red.

"They gave me a lot of money." He was almost yelling, as if he were relaying good news. "For Sveta; when I said that I was her betrothed. Movsar promised me a bride price because Sveta was a virgin when she married him. By accepting the money, I would no longer be her fiancé. I would be innocent, as would Sveta. I discovered that they don't hate Russian women; the very opposite in fact. If you take a Russian wife you prove your bravery. You show your bravery in war with the Russian army. You defeat the Russian army. That's what the people told Movsar. They made a big deal about Sveta. The wedding lasted three days. They boasted that the whole teip was there. That's what they call their clan. Even the oldest of the old men dance. I'm a musician. Chechens don't need anything but Vainakh music, a good horse and a beautiful wife. If you bring home a Russian girl they call you the best Vainakh. They told me that if a Chechen converts his wife to Islam then they are assured passage to paradise."

"Did Sveta promise to convert to Islam?"

Viktor didn't hear my question. His head was hurting again. The pain lasted for a long time, during which he pressed his hands against his head. Once he had regained his composure, I repeated my question.

"I don't know," he replied. "They didn't let me talk to her

for long. Movsar told me 'Friend, if you go near my wife I'll kill you. I'm warning you. That's our adat. Adat is our word for law. Nobody can break the adat. You're Russian. I respect you because you are my wife's older brother. Why did your father betroth you and put earrings in her ears? Sveta told me the whole story in detail. You had to follow Kyrgyz custom. Chechens have the same customs. But a betrothed jigit[2] may not touch the girl until they are married. This is our law.' That's what Movsar told me."

I waved to stop him: "A betrothed girl can't just marry someone else. Why didn't you ask that Chechen why he thought he could violate that custom and marry Sveta?"

"I did ask him, but the old men said that since she's Russian their customs didn't apply. They said that Russians do whatever enters their heads, that in Russia, women choose their husbands. After her marriage Sveta was completely different. She kept a sharp eye on the Chechens. The playful Sveta is gone. Maybe Movsar has put a spell on her. She never shows herself to men. She won't contradict anything her husband says. She never takes the kerchief off her head. Oh Lord!"

"What kind of magic powers does her husband have?" I asked. Unable to contain my anger, I gave a phony smile.

Viktor became excited. "He must have some kind of magic if he turned the head of the girl you were going to marry!"

"Don't link my name with hers! She married your brother Sergei, or have you already forgotten?"

Viktor stared at me without understanding.

"It was a mistake. She should have married you." His regret seemed sincere.

"Don't connect her to me!" I repeated, this time even louder. "She was crazy from the very beginning and she turned

---

2 *Jigit: a skilled and brave equestrian or brave person, in general*

the rest of us into a ridiculous laughing stock all around town. Then there was the fight at her wedding: Your brother's about to go to prison because of that airheaded whore!"

I don't know what thoughts were floating around Viktor's head, but tears suddenly came to his eyes. I was perfectly aware that it was something else, not my words that had made him cry. I needed to get him out of his fog, so I calmly continued:

"You're the older brother, Viktor. Couldn't you have talked to Sveta one more time face to face? I can't believe that the Chechens really won't let her talk to anyone, or was it that Sveta did not want to talk to you?"

"I talked to her. I asked her straight up if that Chechen had put a spell on her. I told her she acts like a doormat when he's about".

"What did she say to that?"

"She said his people are fighting for freedom. They're fighting against tyranny."

"I can't believe your cousin's turned so ideological. She never acted like that before. Or did she?"

"She did, but we never took any notice. She always said, albeit casually, that she didn't want to just live out her life and die at the end. She said she wanted to live a worthy life and die a worthy death. And then she'd laugh."

Inwardly I conceded that generally, people don't remember words like that. But casting my mind back, I realized that Sveta had said similar things to me on many occasions. "How nice", I'd respond, and the words would go in one ear and out the other. They were the kind of grandiose sentiments that no one heeds. People would rather hear a joke, because at least it makes them feel better.

Just then, some doctors entered his room. As I turned to leave, Viktor asked me to wait outside so that he could give me something once they were finished. I nodded and then headed to work on foot. I honestly had no desire to go back into Viktor's hospital room.

I walked along and pondered on why I felt surprised. But no, it wasn't surprise: it was anger. Why are some people so susceptible to ideas that have absolutely nothing to do with them? I decided it must be a form of schizophrenia spread by writers. Just look at Sveta and how she became obsessed with the schizoid ideas of the Chechens. These people have been fighting constantly for a thousand years, waging war and spilling blood in the hope of gaining their freedom. And they have never succeeded: not once! What did that idiot Sveta think she could do? She was a Russian girl. She should have been on the side of her own people, but instead she went and lay under a Chechen! Did she really think that Chechen would appreciate her gesture? I thought of all the stupid women the Chechens had already tortured and made victims of their war. Sveta would just be another victim. They'd brainwash and gang rape her before sticking her full of drugs, tying a grenade to her and yelling "go for it!" The crazy fool would blow up herself and a bunch of her own people. And she deserved it, if she was too stupid to see why the Chechen had lured her to the Caucasus by pretending to be in love with her. She'd die and take some Russians with her. I was sick of reading about it in the paper every day. I was fed up with the terrorists and their brainless shahidki[3]!

I became so agitated that I wasn't even aware of how I arrived at work. My accountant was waiting for me. She reminded me that I had wanted to give Sveta's parents her pay slip as well as the bonus she had earned, and asked me if I was going to call them. I barked at her to call them herself and

---

3 Shahidki: plural for shahidka: an Islamist Chechen female suicide bomber willing to be a martyr in the name of Jihad or Holy War

slammed my door.

A few minutes later the accountant entered my office wide-eyed.

"They don't want Sveta's money. And they don't want to hear her name. They said they never had a daughter by that name."

I was stunned. "Who said that?"

"Both her father and mother."

"I don't believe it."

"Call them yourself."

I thought for a second, but decided I didn't want to call. Why would I? They didn't want to hear about their daughter and what did it have to do with me? She had it coming. More power to them if they'd really disowned her.

* * *

It's hard to be your own judge. I guess I don't have a will of steel. But three days later I found myself standing in front of Viktor. It was cold in his hospital room. The window panes were frosted over. He was covered with a tangle of blankets and other things.

"Why do you keep calling me?" I complained.

He had the covers over his head so that only his eyes shone from underneath. His nostrils exhaled steam. .

"You might not understand Sveta, but she understands you," he replied.

I was overcome by anger. I wanted to turn around and walk out.

"What the hell do I care if she understands me? I don't give a shit!"

He was stubborn. Hiccupping, he went on, "She loves

you for who you are."

I laughed loudly but I was raging inside. "She loves me for who I am but goes and marries another man! I really appreciate her hypocritical love! I've had more than enough of it!"

My feelings were roused. I was furious with Sveta. She should have given her situation more thought earlier in the game before she went and tied her fate and gave up her body to a Chechen. Now it was too late for her regrets.

I waited until my feelings had cooled somewhat and asked a careful, crafty question: "How do you know that she loves me for who I am?"

"It's obvious. Everything's obvious."

"What do you mean?"

Viktor started to gasp for air. He was upset. "You don't get anything, do you? Your face is like glass. Anyone can see what's inside. Just look."

Viktor handed me a photograph. It was a picture of Sveta. She was glowing like the summer sun, even though the picture was taken in the winter against the backdrop of the Caucasus Mountains, covered with fir trees. Her Chechen husband wasn't in the picture so I stared at it for a long time. My eyes hated her, but deep down in my soul something flickered and for an instant, I saw her and the infinite space behind her and felt that I was a wretched beast born of a deceptive dream. Up until that moment, especially during the time I had spent sharing my thoughts with Sveta, I had been confident that I knew who I was. And now this was no longer the case. As God is my witness, I just didn't know anymore. Sveta looked out at me from the photograph and I looked back at her. Perhaps we really did love each other, but it seemed to me that we had always known how different we were in our views and aspirations. I can't say for sure. Maybe Sveta knows who she really is. She probably always knew. But I have to admit that in that instant I didn't recognize myself. I was ashamed of myself. When will the day finally come for all of us to be able to recognize ourselves and develop a true understanding of who we really are? I cannot say.

I suddenly felt tears in my eyes. I hurriedly handed the photo back to Viktor.

He wouldn't take it. "She wanted me to give it to you."

I was taken aback: Should I take it or not? What did I want with it? Why should I have a photo of another man's wife? What kind of trick was life playing on me now?

"The Chechens won't let them live together anyway," Viktor said. He sounded half-asleep.

"Why not?" I was confused.

This is what he told me.

After the wedding the bride and groom had prepared to return home to Kyrgyzstan. However, on the very day that they were supposed to leave, they were summoned to the police station to explain their plans. Once the pair had provided a written explanation, the police made Movsar an offer. They told him that if he stayed in Chechnya he could serve as an officer in a pro-Russian military formation. In fact, they promised to make him a Colonel.

Movsar immediately refused the offer. The police chief demanded to know why. Movsar said that he couldn't take a job that would pit him against the Chechen people's fight for freedom.

"So you're a terrorist! A wolf in sheep's clothing!" accused the chief of police.

"No," Movsar replied. "I married a Russian girl from Kyrgyzstan and we're going back there. I'm not interested in anything else."

Movsar was arrested for treason. Here is a short version of the affidavit Sveta wrote for the police:

"I met Movsar at a dance in Balykchy. I liked him immediately. I can explain why. He's handsome, with shining eyes. I liked how he danced. Nobody could touch him on the dance floor. I could feel his cosmic energy with my whole being. None of my previous boyfriends had energy like that. They were all average people with dim auras and weak bio-energy, but they weren't aware of it. They were cold and dead. None of them could light a fire in my blood and soul or ignite such a volcanic eruption of passion. All of them talked to me with pretentious, empty words: Especially my boss."

When I got to that part, I almost dropped Viktor's laptop on the floor. Shaking with anger, I sat for a long time without reading any further.

"Did you drag this computer all the way from the Caucasus just to show me what that witch wrote about me?" I yelled.

"Don't rush. Keep reading," he said quietly.

I had absolutely no desire to continue reading. To what end? But human fate and human curiosity are strange things. When we watch films we become engrossed in the fate of fictitious people who have nothing to do with us. Perhaps it was for this reason that I resumed reading cautiously. I was somewhat comforted by the thought that if she didn't love me, there was no point in my anguishing over it. I pushed Sveta's image out of my head and read on, as if I were reading about a person I had never met.

"In spite of this, I agreed to marry Sergei Samsonov, a childhood friend from my school days in Balykchy. We had a wedding party. I was wearing a veil and sitting next to Sergei, but my soul was dreaming of Movsar. In my heart I begged his forgiveness for spurning him and marrying Sergei. Three days earlier I had sent Movsar an invitation, even thought I knew he would never come to my wedding. The hardest thing for me to bear was the knowledge that I had cruelly dismissed his pure love as if I had never loved him back. I had trampled on his love which was true and noble. My heart pounded. It told me that no one with a conscience would do what I had done. But it was too late. I couldn't be decisive. I felt sorry for Sergei. I couldn't go against my mother, who had threatened to disown me if I married a Chechen. So instead of being joyful at my wedding I was filled with sorrow. Sergei didn't like my mood. He kept leaving the room. His brother Viktor, on the other hand, liked seeing me upset. As soon as Sergei left, Viktor sat down next to me and asked me if I was sorry to be marrying Sergei. He said it was written on my face. I didn't answer. Viktor was very drunk. He grabbed me by the hand and started whispering to me that I would get tired of Sergei after living with him for a while. Then he sang his song "Beloved" without once taking his eyes off me. All of a sudden Sergei threw a plate in his brother's face and they started fighting. I had been so absorbed by my own worries that I hadn't noticed that the guests were all extremely drunk and that Sergei was high on something. I begged him not to fight. I tried to hold him back. He wouldn't listen to me. There was blood everywhere, dishes flying. I couldn't breathe so I ran outside.

"I believe that I have a guardian angel because I saw Movsar's truck parked under the only working streetlight. I don't remember how I flew to him. I opened the door and saw Movsar inside. He was crying. I just remember telling him to get me out of there.

"I have not withheld anything in this affidavit for the police. I have written down everything exactly as it happened

because I want everyone to know why I did what I did.
Svetlana Danilovna Cherkashina."

Poor Cherkashina's fate was truly tragic. It was worse than a horror film.

"You are Russian. Why is your husband refusing to help the Russians? You are both enemies of the Chechen Republic under the Russian Federation. You pretend to live in Kyrgyzstan but you're both working for the terrorists in secret."

The police made Sveta write another affidavit.

"We married for love. We don't have anything to do with the war. Movsar doesn't support the Russian army or the terrorists because both sides are using force to resolve the conflict. My Movsar is not an officer. He's a musician. He looks at someone and sees only the person they are. If you want to solve the Chechen problem, both sides have to rise above the level of predators and attain truly human qualities. Movsar has often said that the pact between Yeltsin and Maskhadov should never have been broken. I don't know about anything else."

The police psychologist went to Movsar with Sveta's affidavit in hand.

"Your Russian wife has given a statement which claims that you raped her under threat of murder and brought her here from Kyrgyzstan by force. We could turn you over to the Russians for something like that, and you know they won't let you live. If you come over to the Russians' side they'll take any mitigating factors into consideration and may even let you go.

Movsar promised to think it over and give his response in the morning. His relatives were planning to help both of them escape that night. The escape was a failure, and Movsar and Sveta were both recaptured. The Russian administration of Chechnya held them both in custody. That night, Movsar's family paid an enormous bribe, against Sveta's wishes, to the Russian guards. She was released and told to go home to Kyrgyzstan.

Movsar's older brother said to her, "Sister, if my brother's time has come, then he will die. There is no place on this Earth where the bones of Chechens do not lie. But you should live. You bound your life to a son of the Chechens, a Russian woman bound in the sight of God to a Vainakh. By doing so, you gave us at least a small victory in the war. Live well! The Chechen people will not forget you. May Allah be with you! With his help, Movsar will catch up with you in Kyrgyzstan tomorrow. Give him many sons! When they grow up, they will be Vainakhs, born of a Russian mother but ready to give their lives for the freedom of the Chechen people! Each year will bring us more strong, young men!"

With that blessing, Svetlana Cherkashina was escorted by Movsar's younger brother out of Ichkeria, the land declared by Dzhokhar Dudayev which was later destroyed. But she never made it to Kyrgyzstan...

Captain Movsar Baibulayev, currently in custody in Grozny, is an example of the kind of foolish, illiterate people who have come under the influence of Islamic fundamentalists from Afghanistan. Five years ago Baibulayev, who was then a Private in the Russian army, succumbed to the reactionary ideology of the Wahabis and tricked his 15-year-old sister Zeinula into going into the forest with him so that he could rape her. 'Other men will rape you, and it is better that I take your virginity. That is what the Muslim religion demands. Now we are both pure in the eyes of God.' That is how he justified his action to his sister, who lay weeping on the damp ground. Then he handed her over to militants who had come down from the mountains. The whole gang of them raped the girl for two weeks. They beat and brutalized her and then bleached her hair yellow. She lost consciousness, so they pumped her full of drugs. When she came round, they wrapped her in sticks of dynamite and sent her to a Russian army checkpoint to ask for bread. They gave her a cardboard sign that said 'I'm Russian. Please give me bread.' None of the soldiers could bring themselves to shoot the poor girl who came stumbling down the road, and once she got close enough the human bomb detonated. Many of the soldiers were killed. That epitomizes the morals of Chechen militants.

After his sister's death, Private Movsar Baibulayev left his people and country and disappeared without a trace. It was later discovered that he had made his way to distant Kyrgyzstan, where he presented the fake documents of a Russian army officer. He was accepted into the Kyrgyz border service and bought the rank of Captain. After going to such trouble to cover his tracks, the criminal kidnapped a Russian woman named Svetlana Cherkashina on the day of her wedding and took her to Naryn, where he brutally raped her. Then he gave her mood-altering drugs and took her to Chechnya. He was arrested by the patriotic Armed Forces of the Chechen Republic when he attempted to turn the woman over to militants. The investigation is complete and has been turned over to a military judge. During the search, Movsar Baibulayev's laptop computer was seized and found to contain the words of a provocative anti-Chechen song "We'll Come Back to Grozny" by the Wahabi poet Timur Mucuraev. The song is excerpted below:

> Blood red horizon,
> Sun hurrying down,
> Fire licks the sky,
> But Grozny will not fall.
>
> Black craters everywhere,
> Deafening gunfire,
> A child lies bleeding -
> Russian snipers have good aim.

Anger, tears, heartache -
We will avenge ourselves on you!

We leave everything, we slip into the night,
But we'll come back to Grozny!

It's impossible to listen to this gangster poet's nonsense without becoming angry. This so-called song calls for Chechens to revenge themselves on the Russian army, the same army that liberated the Chechen people, who still practice the ancient, brutal custom of blood vengeance.

Chechenskaya Pravda, Stringer news agency.

"After reading the terrible lies about myself and Movsar Baibulayev, I was ill for several days. How could they make up such awful lies about him? I believe that this is an evil worse than any war. It is easier to die from an enemy bullet than bear such black slander.

"Captain Movsar Baibulayev never raped anyone. He still mourns his sister Zeinula, who was pressured by friends to become a shahidka. I have seen the tears in his eyes. I will sue Chechenskaya Pravda. I am a Russian woman from Kyrgyzstan. Chechenskaya Pravda must answer in court for its boldface lies and slander against me."

Svetlana Cherkashina, January 2009. Stringer news agency.

According to Viktor, Cherkashina returned to Grozny the following week. Her customs declaration showed that she had 100 rubles on her, and she listed seeing her husband, Movsar Baibulayev, as the purpose of her trip. She was also carrying papers to file a suit in the city court against Chechenskaya Pravda. While she was waiting in the queue at Customs, she picked up a fresh issue of Chechenskaya Pravda and saw an article entitled "Russian Prostitute Working for Chechen Militants." The article turned out to be a rebuttal of her letter:

Long-time professional prostitute Svetlana Cherkashina entered into a fictitious marriage with Movsar Baibulayev, an underworld agent for Shamil Basayev who went by the name of Wolf. Cherkashina's purpose in Chechnya was to provide assistance to the terrorist Wahabis. At present Cherkashina has plans to file a suit against Chechenskaya Pravda for revealing her actions and her true identity to the world. With this plan in mind, the provocateur published a letter denying her guilt on the Chechenskaya Pravda site. We ask that anyone who sees this woman (photo below) or knows where she is immediately informs the special forces of the Chechen Republic at the following phone number..."

Two days later, news outlets had a new story:

An explosion has been reported at the editorial offices of the liberal newspaper Chechenskaya Pravda. An unidentified shahidka said to have Slavic features, blew herself up at the building. There were no victims, since all of the paper's employees happened to be on break in the smoking lounge.

A medallion bearing the inscription "I will live forever" was found with the shahidka's remains.

Once again the separatist gangsters have shown their bloody hatred for the progressive Chechen people!

* * *

Many years have passed since then. As always, the Chechen people have yet to attain freedom. Sveta is gone. Her true face was gradually erased from my memory. Only sorrow and pity – complex, ambiguous feelings – were left in my soul. It is hard to understand what someone is thinking when she tries to defend her desecrated honour by going to a voluntary death, after which she hopes to attain eternal life. Who knows? I can't say for sure. Maybe that was the right thing for her to do. Maybe Svetlana was right all along: Because only the living can attain their earthly aims!

**"Thirteen Steps towards the Fate of Erika Klaus"
by the National Writer of Kyrgyzstan,
Kazat Akmatov**

Is set in a remote outpost governed by a fascist regime, based on real events in a mountain village in Kyrgyzstan ten years ago. It narrates challenges faced by a young, naïve Norwegian woman who has volunteered to teach English. Immersed in the local community, her outlook is excitable and romantic until she experiences the brutal enforcement of the political situation on both her own life and the livelihood of those around her. Events become increasingly violent, made all the more shocking by Akmatov's sensitive descriptions of the magnificent landscape, the simple yet proud people and their traditional customs.

Born in 1941 in the Kyrgyz Republic under the Soviet Union, Akmatov has first -hand experience of extreme political reactions to his work which deemed anti-Russian and anti-communist, resulted in censorship. Determined to fight for basic human rights in oppressed countries, he was active in the establishment of the Democratic Movement of Kyrgyzstan and through his writing, continues to highlight problems faced by other central Asian countries.

RRP:£12.95
ISBN: 978-0955754951

Friendly Steppes: A Silk Road Journey
by Nick Rowan

This is the chronicle of an extraordinary adventure that led Nick Rowan to some of the world's most incredible and hidden places. Intertwined with the magic of 2,000 years of Silk Road history, he recounts his experiences coupled with a remarkable realisation of just what an impact this trade route has had on our society as we know it today. Containing colourful stories, beautiful photography and vivid characters, and wrapped in the local myths and legends told by the people Nick met and who live along the route, this is both a travelogue and an education of a part of the world that has remained hidden for hundreds of years.

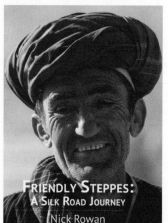

Friendly Steppes: A Silk Road Journey reveals just how rich the region was both culturally and economically and uncovers countless new friends as Nick travels from Venice through Eastern Europe, Iran, the ancient and modern Central Asia of places like Samarkand, Bishkek and Turkmenbashi, and on to China, along the Silk Roads of today.

RRP:£14.95
ISBN: 978-0-9557549-4-4

When The Edelweiss Flowers Flourish
by Begenas Sartov

The author frequently explored the tension between Soviet technological progress, the political and social climates and Kyrgyz traditions in his work, and When The Edelweiss Flowers Flourish depicts an uneasy relationship between two worlds.

Using the science fiction genre, the novel's main character is Melis – derived from Marx, Engels, Lenin and Stalin – who has his counter in Silem, an alien being sent to earth to remove Edelweiss plants to help save his own planet from a deadly virus.

The essence of the story was attributed by Begenas to a childhood experience when a village elder helped him recuperate from breaking his arm, using a herbal mixture of seven grasses. These grasses – Edelweiss, Ermen, Ak kadol, Shyraajyn, Oo koroshyn, Kokomirin and Shybak – are still found in the high Kyrgyz mountains today, and are still widely used for their medicinal properties.

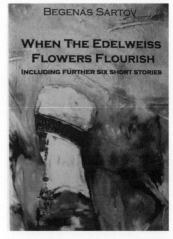

RRP:£12.95
ISBN: 978-0955754951

Birds of Uzbekistan
by Boris Nedosekov

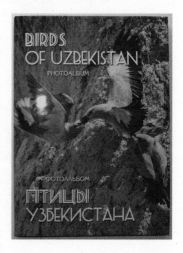

This is a superb collection of full-colour photographs provided by the members of Uzbekistan Society for the Protection of Birds, with text in both English and in Russian. Since the collapse of the Soviet Union and Uzbekistan's declaration of independence in 1991, unlike in other Central Asian states there have been no such illustrated books published about the birds of this country's rich and diverse wildlife.

There are more than 500 species of birds in Uzbekistan, with 32 included in the International Red Data Book. After independence, Uzbekistan began to attract the attention of foreign tourist companies, and particularly those specialising in ornithological tourism and birdwatching.

Birds of Uzbekistan is therefore a much-needed and timely portrait of this element of the country's remarkable wildlife.

RRP: £24.95
ISBN: 978-0955754913

Under the Wolf nest: A Turkic Rhapsody
by Kairat Zakiryanov

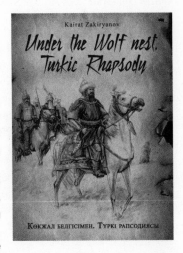

Were the origins of Islam, Christianity and the legend of King Arthur all influenced by steppe nomads from Kazakhstan?

Ranging through thousands of years of history, and drawing on sources from Herodotus through to contemporary Kazakh and Russian research, the crucial role in the creation of modern civilisation played by the Turkic people is revealed in this detailed yet highly accessible work.

Professor Kairat Zakiryanov, President of the Kazakh Academy of Sport and Tourism, explains how generations of steppe nomads, including Genghis Khan, have helped shape the language, culture and populations of Asia, Europe, the Middle East and America through migrations taking place over millennia.

History is shaped by the victors, but after the collapse of the Soviet Union new attempts are being made to recover historical and ethnographical detail that previous empires swept aside. After reading Under the Sign of the Wolf: A Turkic Rhapsody you will look again at language and culture, and realise the living histories they represent.

RRP: £ 17.50
ISBN: 978-0957480728

Tales from Bush House
collected and edited by Hamid Ismailov,
Marie Gillespie, and Anna Aslanyan

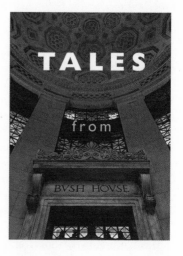

This is a collection of short narratives about working lives, mostly real and comic, sometimes poignant or apocryphal, gifted to the editors by former and current BBC World Service employees. They are tales from inside Bush House – the home of the World Service since 1941 – escaping through its marble-clad walls at a time when its staff members began their departure to new premises in Portland Place.

In its collective authorship, it documents the cultural diversity of the World Service, showing how the extraordinary people who worked there, and the magnificent, chaotic building they shared, shaped one another. We use the word tales to signal that this is a book that mixes genres – ethnographic and folkloric stories, oral histories and jokes. Recounting tales involves an intricate relationship between talking and telling – as in the working life of a broadcaster.

RRP: £ 12.50
ISBN: 978-0-9557549-7-5

Igor Savitsky: Artist, Collector, Museum Founder
by Marinika Babanazarova

This is the biography of the astonishing life of Igor Savitsky, who rescued thousands of dissident artworks from Stalinist repression that survive today in the Karakalpakstan Museum, in Nukus, Uzbekistan; a collection of Soviet avant-garde art rivalled only by the Russian Museum in St Petersburg. The remoteness of the area, and its proximity to chemical weapons testing sites nearby, helped Savitsky keep his collection secret while, tragically, some of the Russian and Uzbek artists involved were either imprisoned or executed.

The author is the director of the museum, a post she has held since the death in 1984 of Savitsky, who was a regular visitor to her family. Savitsky's life is vividly narrated through detail from correspondence, official records, and family documents that have become available only recently, as well as the recollections of so many of those who knew this remarkable man.

RRP:£10.00
ISBN: 978-0-9557549-9-9

THE ALPHABET GAME
by Paul Wilson

Paul Wilson has been travel writing for over twenty years, and is a leading light on The Silk Road, past and present. He has also written a play: Shakespeare Tonight. If it is raining in Macclesfield, Paul can be found in Sydney, with his wife and son. With the future of Guidebooks under threat, The Alphabet Game takes you back to the very beginning, back to their earliest incarnations and the gamesmanship that brought them into being. As Evelyn Waugh's Scoop did for Foreign Correspondents the world over, so this novel lifts the lid on Travel Writers for good. Travelling around the world may appear as easy as A,B,C in the twenty first century, but looks can be deceptive: there is no 'X' for a start. Not since Xidakistan was struck from the map. But post 9/11, with the War on Terror going global, the sovereignty of 'The Valley' is back on the agenda. Could the Xidakis, like their Uzbek and Tajik neighbours, be about to taste the freedom of independence? Will Xidakistan once again take its rightful place in the League of Nations? The Valley's fate is inextricably linked with that of Graham Ruff, founder of Ruff Guides. In a tale setting sail where Around the World in Eighty Days and Lost Horizon weighed anchor, our not-quite-a-hero suffers all the slings and arrows outrageous fortune can muster, in his pursuit of the golden triangle: The Game, The Guidebook, The Girl. Wilson tells The Game's story with his usual mix of irreverent wit and historical insight, and in doing so delivers the most telling satire on an American war effort since M*A*S*H. The Guidebook is Dead? Long Live the Guidebook.

Available on pre-order
E-mail: publisher@ocamagazine.com
Publisher: Hertfordshire press (March 2014), paperback
RRP: £14.95

THE GODS OF THE MIDDLE WORLD
by Galina Dolgaya

The Gods of the Middle World, the new novel by Galina Dolgaya, tells the story of Sima, a student of archaeology for whom the old lore and ways of the Central Asian steppe peoples are as vivid as the present. When she joints a group of archaeologists in southern Kazakhstan, asking all the time whether it is really possible to 'commune with the spirits', she soon discovers the answer first hand, setting in motion events in the spirit worlds that have been frozen for centuries. Meanwhile three millennia earlier, on the same spot, a young woman and her companion struggle to survive and amend wrongs that have caused the neighbouring tribe to avenge for them. The two narratives mirror one another, while Sima finds her destiny intertwined with the struggle between the forces of good and evil. Drawing richly on the historical and mythical backgrounds of the southern Kazakh steppe, the novel ultimately addresses the responsibilities of each generation for those that follow and the central importance of love and forgiveness.

Based in Tashkent and with a lifetime of first-hand knowledge of the region in which the story is set, Galina Dolgaya has published a number of novels and poems in Russian. The Gods of the Middle World won first prize at the 2012 Open Central Asia Literature Festival and is her first work to be available in English, published by Hertfordshire Press.

Available on pre-order
E-mail: publisher@ocamagazine.com
Publisher: Hertfordshire press (March 2014), paperback
RRP: £14.95

100 EXPERIENCES OF KYRGYZSTAN
Text by Ian Claytor

You would be forgiven for missing the tiny landlocked country of Kyrgyzstan on the map. Meshed into Central Asia's inter-locking web of former Soviet Union boundaries, this mountainous country still has more horses than cars. It never fails to surprise and delight all who visit. Proud of its nomadic traditions, dating back to the days of the Silk Road, be prepared for Kyrgyzstan's overwhelming welcome of hospitality, received, perhaps, in a shepherd's yurt out on the summer pastures. Drink bowls of freshly fermented mare's milk with newfound friends and let the country's traditions take you into their heart. Marvel at the country's icy glaciers, crystal clear lakes and dramatic gorges set beneath the pearly white Tien Shan mountains that shimmer, heaven-like, in the summer haze as the last of the winter snows caps their dominating peaks. Immerse yourself in Central Asia's jewel with its unique experiences and you will leave with a renewed zest for life and an unforgettable sense of just how man and nature can interact in harmony.

ISBN: 978-0-9574807-4-2
RRP: £14.95